# THE FEATHERED THRONE

# The Feathered Throne

Alaina Paul

# Contents

# 1

# Jarren

"Please," she begged, screaming and thrashing her body against the cloaked figure. "You can't do this! He's just a boy! My poor boy." She sobbed as they ripped the young child away and carried him up the road, heading towards the rising sun behind the castle walls.

Jarren watched in horror, as he had done countless times before. He breathed slowly in and out, trying to calm his racing heart. The woman fell to the ground, sobbing with her face pressed against the muddy road. His whole body was tense, almost shaking as he exhaled a sigh, a feeling of helplessness taking over him. He ducked back down among the profusely overgrown shrubbery, melding into the surrounding thickets. The trees here grew too closely together, obscuring the sun above the thick foliage canopy, twisting and turning to fight their way to the top. It was as though even the trees here were fighting to free themselves from within the cities' walls.

*Clip-clop-clip-clop.* He closed his eyes, straining his ears to fixate on the sounds of the nearing horse's hooves pounding against the densely packed dirt. Gradually, the sound began to rise above the rhythmic cacophony surrounding him. It cut through the shrill chorus of the woman's cries. Inhale. Exhale.

He looked up and saw a streak of black sweeping through the trees, nearing the bend in the road. He tightened his grip around his dagger, watching as two charcoal black horses emerged from around the bend and trotted into view. He squinted at the men riding them, scanning slowly up and down. Their full black attire made them unmistakable; only the Black Cloaks were allowed to cover their faces. He scowled and ducked back further into the shrubbery, listening to their chattering voices. They laughed as they passed by the weeping woman. They were heartless, cold, and seemed almost excited by others' suffering. He grimaced and inched back haltingly, fearing the slightest misstep might alert them of his lingering presence. And then, just as suddenly as he arrived, he disappeared behind the forest's wooden walls.

When he was certain he could no longer hear hooves pounding, he began running back towards the city's outskirts, as he had done daily for the past week. The sun climbed into the morning sky and cascaded colors across the clouds. He wondered how terror had filled the air just moments ago, and now it was as if the world had simply moved on and forgotten the monstrosities the morning brought.

He finally slowed when he reached the sight of the dark stone wall surrounding the city. Gradually, his breath began to slow as he trudged along the edge of the wall. He ran his hand gently across the cracked and broken brick surface, feeling the rough, worn-down texture scrape against the pads of his fingers.

He slipped down a narrow alleyway and was thrown out into a bustling street brimming with every sort of person there was. He pushed past people bickering over land, food, water, and anything people could fight over. He slipped through gaps between buildings and ducked under makeshift clotheslines, trying to get through without drawing any unnecessary attention. Mourner's Row grew increasingly crowded each year, and the streets seemed to grow smaller. He could feel the palpable growing tension in the air; a wave of unease settled somewhere deep inside him. He suffocated in a sea of people surrounding him, pushed this way and that by an undertow of strangers. Soon, he reached the only home he'd ever known, a small three-room house on the edge of town, pressed against one of the city walls.

He knocked on the doorway as he entered the dark brown building, more out of habit than anything else. His father's sighing face came into view as he shuffled into the room. He was sitting at his desk, surrounded by papers and shelves overflowing with odds and ends. His bright blond hair stuck out against the background of maps and reports haphazardly arranged upon the grim, dark walls behind him, lit only by a few candles.

"Did you see them again today?" Rowan asked. He glanced up at him expectantly, his cold blue eyes showing no sign of emotion, his hand still writing on a sheet of paper.

"Yes, around the same time, too," Jarren replied hesitantly.

He knew this would upset his father and that frequent trips by the Black Cloaks could only mean one thing. He wished that he hadn't seen them, that they hadn't ridden past him. He wished that he still believed the walls around him could protect him. But, most of all, he wished that there was something, anything, he could do to stop what he knew was inevitably coming.

Rowan sighed and shook his head as he went back to his papers. The last thing he needed was confirmation of what he already suspected. Their brief reprieve of peace would soon be gone. Whether it was at the hands of rioters or Black Cloaks hardly made a difference, although they each seemed equally likely, almost as though it was merely a race between the two. He shuffled papers around his desk, pushing stacks around the already cluttered surface, somehow managing to avoid the inevitable occurrence of the papers crashing to the ground they desperately edged towards.

"I'll call a meeting tonight, and we'll discuss the matter," he huffed.

Jarren left with that, knowing there was nothing he could do to help put his father's mind at ease. Anything he elaborated on would only cause him further consternation. So he wandered back through the crowded streets and toward the Southern corner of the wall. Gradually, the noise of the busy streets grew softer, the paths spread wider, and the air smelled more of dirt and salt water.

"What took you so long?" Ezra asked.

He stopped abruptly as his eyes darted up. He sighed in relief as he saw her fiery auburn hair peeking through the light green leaves around her. "I... I got caught up," he mumbled.

Ezra was always perched here and there, in one tree or another. He had asked her about it years before, and she claimed she somehow felt safer in the air. But, of course, they both were keenly aware that it offered no protection at all; however, the false sense of safety was still very much real to them. Thus, they had spent their lives up in the trees, giving them at least some feeling of control over their own safety.

"What happened? Did they come again?"

"No, no, nothing like that. I just got distracted; I have a lot on my mind. Us peasants don't have the easiest life, you know," he lied as he carefully placed his foot on a low-hanging branch, slowly making his way up the tree across from her.

"At least you aren't forced to dine alongside the royal family. I'd much rather be climbing out here with you than watching my parents exchange subtle threats and baiting one another over supper."

"I'm quite sure listening to political discussions during meals must be maddening. I can't fathom how your parents put up with the Queen or her little puppet. If I were in the same room with her, I'd kill her the first chance I got."

"Well then... I guess it's good that *my* father is a lord and *not* yours," she snarked.

"Well, I think it would be quite amusing to be a lord," he said matter-of-factly. "Watching all the other lords drink themselves to death at every feast. Having every lady in the land throwing themselves at my feet."

"No lady would want you even if you were a lord," she laughed, "You're much too arrogant even now."

He scoffed and darkened his gaze as he watched her mock him. "At least I would make something of myself. I would be a contributing member of my family. You take every chance you can to sneak away and climb trees, eavesdropping and spying on people all the time."

She gasped and smiled, placing her hand on her chest. "How dare you insinuate such things! I am not spying on people; I am simply watching people who aren't aware of it," she corrected.

"You can call it what you want, but I know spying when I see it. Speaking of… anything good today?"

He laid down across a large tree branch, his back resting against the top of the tree,

"Well, let's see… Mr. Armitage and the farmers delivered another load of squash, and one of Darby's boys fell and broke his wrist. Mr. Smythe visited the brothel again, too," she said triumphantly.

"Wow," he chuckled. "It's been a rather busy morning."

"Yes, quite. What about you? Anything… new?"

His smile faded, and he stared down at the brick wall. He knew what she was really asking.

"My father's calling a meeting tonight to discuss what we'll do next."

"Oh," she said after a short silence, her voice suddenly quiet. "They did come today… didn't they? We went weeks without incident. And now it's even worse than it was before. More and more people are being carted away, beaten, killed… No one can stop the Black Cloaks, and they know it. If they label anyone unfaithful, they can do as they please with them. No one can protect the weak and innocent. Not even my father."

He turned to look at her and watched as her eyes darted around, refusing to look at him. He saw her once bright smile fade into a taut line as she played with the edge of her recently torn dress.

"Ezra…"

"No, no… I'm fine. I just wish there was something we could do about it," she replied, now fidgeting with a leaf next to her.

Jarren sighed and turned to face her. "I know you're afraid, and I understand why, but they're getting increasingly violent, and soon it will no longer be safe here."

Ezra glared at him and tossed the leaf down to the ground. Her fair skin was flushed red, and her amber-brown eyes began to well with tears.

"No, you don't understand. You don't understand what it's like to sit right next to evil and be unable to do anything about it. You don't understand sitting there and shaking with fear, praying you won't say the wrong thing, and ending up dead. You have no idea what living in the same castle as those monsters is like. I can't say anything to anyone in there, not even my own family. You don't know what it's like to grow up alone in a world like this. I'll never be safe; none of us will."

He sighed and looked into her teary brown eyes as he tried to concoct a reply that wouldn't anger her further.

"You're right. I don't know what it was like for you, and I'm sorry. But I do know this... Every day, Queen Arabella grows stronger, and the Black Cloaks hurt more and more people. She rules with fear and intimidation, and she knows that won't last forever. The people will rise up, and she knows it. She'll try to kill every traitor and anyone even suspected of rebelling. And sooner or later, they'll find us, and I won't be here waiting for them when they do. We can't just do nothing, and you know that... So don't throw your life away sitting up in this tree, afraid to do anything."

She sniffled and fidgeted with her hands, focusing on them instead of him. He knew she was listening to what he was saying, but he also knew fear was stronger than logic. He, of all people, understood that the days of relative peace were quickly coming to an end.

"I know. I guess it's just easy to get caught up in the grim of it all. We grew up hearing tales of what it was like before us, how perfect it seems compared to this, and I know we'll never have that. But the comfort of these trees, being outside the castle walls and away from it all. There's nowhere I'd rather be. No matter how fleeting, it's as close to perfect as it will ever be," she replied.

"All that matters is that at this moment, we're safe. Besides, we'll always have each other," he said with a small smile.

He had never meant to upset her and had never seen her this disquieted. She had expressed these fears and worries before, but the recent immediacy of discovery had only worsened them. Everybody was on edge these days, almost as though they were losing a battle in their minds before the true battle had even begun.

"I guess that's better than most," she said as she looked up at him.

"You deserve better than most," he replied earnestly.

"Let's go before they come looking for me." She began climbing down the tree, a small smile overtaking her face.

"I'll race you home," he challenged.

"You don't have a chance," she warned, taking off towards the city.

He was glad that she seemed to have listened to him. He never wanted to upset her, only prepare her for whatever everyone knew was coming. He felt as though he could sense it in the air. Something dark, cold, was approaching. He felt it in the crispness of the air and the stirring of the leaves. Something dreadful was coming, and he didn't like it.


Jarren plopped down against the side of the drinking fountain, pulling a stale piece of bread from his pant pocket. He rested his head back against the cold stone and looked out over the garden. Plants, herbs, and flowers of all types lined the land, distinguishing it from the rest of the city. Somehow, among all the chaos, here stood this beautiful place. He thought back to his stories and dreams of adventure and wondered if there were places in the world that were as peaceful as this place appeared to be. He could hardly imagine a place that wasn't as foul and filthy as Vaor. He dreamed that one day he could see such a place if it did exist.

Across from him stood a church, tall and statuesque. It stood proudly as the sun set behind him, the garden trees and bushes casting shadows upon its white walls. He exhaled a sigh, a sense of peace washing over him. A few women passed by, heading in to offer more daily prayers to the Gods. They placed their coins in The Dove's fountain for protection and dropped their blood into The Raven's pool for protection, as if he could save them from the terrors of this world.

He stood and sipped the cold water from the spout. A small stream poured down below the carving of a raven and a dove perched on a tree branch. He shook his head slightly as if to wake his mind up from a dream. He walked slowly back through the streets and watched as they turned from the tradesman and the shops to the taverns and the brothels and finally to the outskirts of the city. He made his way past the houses long forgotten and the people with them until he finally reached his father's door. He paused slightly before creaking open the door and tiptoeing to the back room. He tried not to disturb his father, tonight's gathering looming over his thoughts.

"Where were you off to this time?" Rowan questioned from his desk.

He paused and turned to face his father, dreading the conversation he knew was coming. "I was just talking to Ezra, that's all," he replied coolly.

"You know how I feel about you wasting time with her. Now that you're older, you should have more responsibilities instead of running off with her every chance you get. She's dangerous. We've spoken about this before."

"I know," Jarren said defeatedly.

"You have to prepare for what's to come. Each minute you waste could be the difference between life and death. You, of all people, should know this." He huffed, leaning back in his chair. "The meeting starts in a few minutes, so change out of those dirty clothes."

Jarren trudged to his room and closed the door, wanting to slam it but knowing better. His room had nothing to show, the same as everywhere in Mourner's Row. It was big enough for a small bed and a bookshelf filled with a few trinkets and books he had collected over the years. These few possessions fed into his fantasy life, nagging on his dreams of adventure, heroism, and far-off places. They gave him hope of one day living out his fantasy. He dreamt most nights of becoming one of the heroes he had read about. Saving villages from tyranny and rising up against the unjust. He frequently caught himself tangled up inside one of his visions, forcing himself to remember that those were only stories.

He begrudgingly changed into a more appropriate outfit and lined up a few chairs. He had been tasked with this mundane job ever since he was a child because he was the son of the rebellion's leader, and that was his job. He had to train hard, work even harder, and become the perfect man to help lead the revolution with his father. As he monotonously completed the chore, his thoughts drifted back to his childhood. Always studying maps and strategies, never being allowed to play or cause trouble. *"You can't be seen frolicking about and flying off the handle. How can people expect your father to lead everyone if he can't even control you?"* His mother had said to him.

The only reprieve he had was the time he spent with Ezra. She was free-spirited, kind, and much smarter than he was, which he knew, although he would never admit to it. He smiled at the thought of her, then was pulled from his thoughts by a knock at the door.

He quickly answered it before returning to his task, hurrying to finish setting up the maps as people entered the room. They chattered amongst themselves impatiently as they waited anxiously to hear the news. A dozen or so people lined up around the room's walls, packed into corners, and squashed into seats to accommodate everyone.

"Thank you for coming." Rowan stood from his desk as the chattering died down. "As you know, my son has been traveling up the road daily to keep track of the Black Cloaks location. This past week, they have passed by every morning. They've been scouring the area far more frequently than we've previously seen. They have also been seen taking more and more prisoners to be interrogated at the castle. It seems Queen Arabella grows more wary of a rebellion forming since the news of the uprising on the war front. Even though her troops are spread thin, she has sent the Black Cloaks back into the streets.

For now, we will not interfere and instead wait until we know anything further. I know many of you spend your nights worrying about our discovery and capture. I urge you to remember that we have hidden away here for many years now, safely. Once we have word of an opportunity to gain control of the castle and capture the Queen, we will make our move. But, until then, we must wait. Patience is our strength. Your continued faith in me will carry us through these hardships."

Rowan stepped back and began walking towards the door. People shouted questions over each other and forced their way towards the door, nudging and elbowing others out of the way, trying to catch up to him. He was a somewhat convincing speaker, but people knew the truth: he couldn't do anything to protect them. Jarren knew better than to ask for promises of safety that he knew his father couldn't keep.

"An excellent meeting, wouldn't you say?" Evelyn asked, a small smile on her face.

"Yes, Mother," he replied instinctively as he watched the horde pour through the doors.

"I think your father handled that well considering the circumstances, don't you?"

"I suppose." Jarren shrugged.

Everyone had filed out of the room by now, leaving them in an uncomfortably long silence. The enveloping sound of rain thrumming against the roof grumbled in the background.

"Speaking of your father, he has organized another run later this week." She brushed her curly, light brown hair out of her face as she watched his reaction.

"Again? We just did a trip a few weeks ago," Jarren asked incredulously.

"Well...with the Black Cloaks causing as much trouble as they have, he says we need eyes inside the castle. We need to know what's to come in order to prepare."

"That's precisely the reason we shouldn't go. Black Cloaks are everywhere these days. Sneaking inside the castle is more dangerous than ever." He stared with fire in his eyes.

"It's your father's decision. I won't argue with you."

"Which unlucky man was coerced into going this time?" he asked.

"We were planning on sending the Darby boys; however, Jonah just broke his wrist and isn't able to go. I remembered that I hadn't gone for some time, so I volunteered."

Jarren's gaze shot up to meet her uncertain brown eyes. "Are you trying to get yourself killed? Why would you volunteer? It's too dangerous! And how did you get Father to agree to this?" he asked with disbelief, his heart racing in anger.

"I won't be going alone; Merric will be accompanying me; that's the only reason your father is letting me go. I'll be in good hands, so there's no need to worry about me. He would never allow me to go if he thought I would be in danger," she insisted.

"Evelyn!" Rowan interrupted.

"I'm sorry, we'll finish this discussion later," she mumbled apologetically as she hurried outside.

As much as Jarren wanted to be upset by his mother's abrupt ending to the conversation, he knew it was rather typical of her to do so. Unfortunately, confrontation wasn't something this family deemed a worthwhile activity. It was apparently decided years ago that unpleasantness had no place in a family surrounded by a rather unpleasant world.

He walked over to the doorway and peered into a blanket of darkness surrounding him. Rain cut through the sky and clattered onto the ground, diving down and breaking free from the thick gray ceiling. Screams erupted from the streets outside, and his annoyance was immediately washed away as he ran outside, unsure of what to do. The air buzzed frantically around him, and the hair on his arms stood up in anticipation. He watched fearfully as people shouted at one another, grabbing their loved ones and fleeting into their houses. He scoured the area, running to the densely crowded spot in the streets. Flames engulfed a building further down the way as horses neighed in the distance. He glanced up and saw his father's panicked expression. Jarren followed his eyes and traced them back to his mother's pale, wide-eyed face.

"Rioters," she trembled. "May the gods help us all."

# 2

# Ezra

She padded down the stone corridor, breathing slowly with each step. She ran her hand along the edge of the wall, using it to guide her through the pitch-black walkway. After countless times using this castle exit, she had memorized each stone carving, every statue, and every archway in her path. She breathed a sigh of relief when she felt her hand make contact with the far wall. She slowly tiptoed up the spiraling staircase and made her way up from the crypt below. She paused near the top of the stairs, listening for confirmation before continuing through the archway.

"Sneaking off again, I see." A tall figure said, peeking around the corner.

"Don't you have training to do?" Ezra replied with a huff. She rolled her eyes and turned to face him. His features mimicked her own: curly red hair, a tall, slender figure, and freckles. Their resemblance was unmistakable, although they couldn't have been further apart.

"I finished already with the swordsman. Father and I are leaving on a hunt tomorrow. I thought I would come and admire your needlepoint work. That's when I found out you'd snuck off again," Taenin replied with a smirk.

"Admire my needlework? You mean to say that you were coming to check up on me. To make sure I hadn't left again."

"You can imagine my immense surprise then to find out you had," he countered.

"I wasn't gone for too long. Besides, I was careful not to be seen. I just needed an hour or so outside the castle. A chance to clear my head, that's all."

"Oh, I'm certain that's all it was. I was able to track your secret entryway easily enough. I'm sure it won't be long until someone else discovers your passageway."

"Please don't tell father… He hates it when I sneak out," Ezra pleaded.

"I'm afraid he already knows. Marcella came to ask if he'd seen you."

The darkness in the hallway didn't cover up the dread that flashed across her face. She had known the risk of getting caught each time she left, although she rarely ever was. Still, she knew that she would be put on lockdown each time and watched day and night by her handmaiden. That, however, wasn't the worst part she knew she had to endure. The part she hated the most was the lecture she knew was to come from her father.

She slowly made her way through the winding halls until she reached his quarters at the far side of the castle. His door was cracked open, and she heard a fireplace crackling softly from within. She breathed in one final deep breath before pushing through the doorway and looking up to meet her father's gaze.

He immediately launched into his usual spiel of her lack of maturity and flagrant displays of rebellion. Nevertheless, she was glad that her family had come to visit her in the Capital, although she could do without his tedious lectures.

She stared at the honeycomb brown walls behind him, finding the cracks running through the bricks more interesting than the conversation she was having with him. Rows of blood-red banners hung proudly along the walls, overpowering the mostly barren room. The King and Queen were anything but subtle. She scoffed at their blatant overcompensation; her home further South was nothing like the castle here in Vaor. She hadn't been back home for some time, and she wondered whether or not it still looked like what she remembered.

"Ezra!" He slammed his palm against the dark wooden table, causing it to shake from the force. "Listen to me."

Her head snapped up to look at her father. His eyes were blazing brown, and he stared deep into her eyes.

"As I was saying, now is not the time for frolicking around the city grounds. It's not safe out there for young girls, even less so for a lady. So I will not have you sneaking out of the castle anymore!"

"I'm sorry, Father. I know I shouldn't have snuck off again. I just wanted to-."

"Enough," Lord Gareth said. "Your mother and I decided years ago that you desperately needed structure and guidance. You are a *lady*; you will learn to act like one. We sent you here in hopes that it would end your disobedience. However, you have taken every chance to disobey our wishes. Your brother and I are leaving for another hunt tomorrow. After we return, we are leaving back to Rivers End. You are to remain here in-"

"But Father! You promised me that I could come home!" She shook, her voice wavering. She stood from her chair, looking down upon her father's gray hair.

"Ezra, your brother is the heir to Rivers End. It is his duty to take my place. You are growing older, and soon you will need to marry-"

"Father, please don't make me stay!" she begged, burying her freckled face into her hands.

He stood up from the table and wrapped her in his arms, his voice calming at the sight of her. "I take no pleasure in sending my only daughter away. But, you must understand, I have no choice in the matter. You must learn to be a lady if you wish to marry."

"I don't want to marry. I want to be free. I want to travel the world."

"That isn't your choice to make," he sighed. "You are my daughter; therefore, you must marry into a noble family. You don't have to like it, but it must be done."

"Father... please don't make me stay," she whimpered.

"From this moment forward, you are to remain within the castle walls at all times. Marcella will watch over you and report back to me if you are to sneak out again." He placed his hand under her chin and lifted it to meet his eyes. "I will not hear from her again, do you understand?"

"Yes, Father."


She trudged into her bedroom in the far tower of the castle. It was a small room with a window facing the streets below. A fireplace sat on the southern wall, and a bed was pushed up against the wall beside it. A table sat in the center of the room, topped with a small platter of fruit and cheeses. A dresser sat beside the door, filled with dresses of all different colors. The bedding and silk curtains were made with a deep red fabric embellished with a swirling gaudy gold. She detested the opulence that the King and Queen surrounded themselves with almost as much as she hated the extravagant gowns she was forced to wear. The only time she enjoyed herself in the Capital was when she was with Jarren. He never treated her like she was any different than he was. Everyone here was much too proper and formal.

She walked over to her large windows overlooking the city. Tall, dark roofs rose from the ground all around her, creating a layer of mismatched brown draping across the area. She watched as hundreds of commoners walked around the streets of Vaor, only tiny specks from where she was standing. Large gray towers stuck out of the ground like spikes, and walls wrapped along the outskirts of the city, separating them from the brutal world beyond the walls. Distancing them from everything and everyone beyond.

"Ezra, where were you?" Marcella asked.

She turned to face her handmaiden walking into the room, her eyebrows knit together, and her mouth pulled into a deep frown.

"I just returned from a rather bland lecture from my father. He's decided to keep me here indefinitely," she muttered. "At least until I am to marry."

"I'm sorry," Marcella replied. "I never meant to get you into trouble. I know how badly you wished to return home."

Ezra sighed and studied her up and down. She looked beautiful in her flowy pink dress. Her light blonde hair and large green eyes sparkled in the soft light shining through the window. She yearned to trade places with her. Then, she wouldn't be held back by the frivolous rules and responsibilities of nobility.

"Father says I'm to marry soon," she stated, a blank expression on her face.

"I'm sure he'll select a fine young man for you. Someone who will take you somewhere beautiful, somewhere far away. He'll find you someone handsome and wonderful, I'm sure of it."

"I do not wish to be someone else's property." She turned back to look out over the city. "I don't want to marry, whether he's handsome or not."

Ezra knew this was her duty. She was to marry a lord and keep his house. She would bear his children, just as her mother had done before her.

Marcella paused and walked over to stand behind her. She faced her and offered a small smile as she spoke. "He will romance you and take you away, and you will grow to love him. He will treat you well, and you shall be happy. That is the way it works. Many of us aren't so fortunate."

Ezra returned a small smile before turning away to lie on her bed. A tear began to well in her eyes, and her body ached at the thought of remaining here.

"I wish to rest until supper time," she dismissed, her voice trembling and weak.

"As you wish," Marcella replied.

An array of exotic fruits, wines, meats, and cheeses spilled over the silver platters lining the table before her. She sat beside her father, who was seated opposite King Henry. Queen Arabella, her son, her daughter, and the rest of Ezra's family were situated around the table. A silence lulled over the hall as they scraped at their plates. Candlelight flickered on their faces and wrapped the room in a false sense of comfort. Supper with the King and Queen was something she dreaded each day, even more so now that she knew she was being forced to stay.

"Here, boy, another glass of wine," The King called to one of his servants. "I suppose I can't convince you to stay, Gareth?"

"My people need me, Your Grace."

"And your daughter, she's to remain here?" he asked, wine dribbling down the wiry gray hair feathering his chin.

"We believe it's for the best," Lady Kira said.

The King took a slow sip of wine as he stared at Ezra. She quickly glanced down at her plate and picked at the grapes in front of her.

"I believe it's about time we have your daughter wed, Gareth. I see no reason not to make the match myself, seeing I've practically raised her these past few years."

Her eyes met his gaze at this revelation, only to find that he was no longer looking at her. She could think of countless reasons why she shouldn't be matched, even more so now that he wanted to be the one to do it.

"Your Grace, I-" Lord Gareth started.

"She shall wed my son, Oliver, when the time comes."

Ezra froze, the grape she was fiddling with slipping through her fingers and landing on her plate. She slowly raised her eyes to the young man sitting across from her. He was the striking image of his mother. He had dark amber hair and eyes to match, with a harsh bone structure and broad shoulders. She had always found him quite handsome, like many other young maidens. Still, the thought of marrying him repulsed her to her core. He was the picture of grace and nobility, never once forgetting his manners. He always knew what to say and do, the perfect young man. He was older than she was by quite a few years. She supposed that was why she had never thought of this possibility before. He was a man of honor, and she was a young girl. He was also the worst possible match for her, she thought. It would make her Queen one day, and she would remain trapped in this castle forever.

Lady Kira gasped, hesitating before she spoke, "Henry, it would be an honor to join our two families, no doubt. However... I do believe the ceremony should wait to take place until Spring. Winter is fast approaching, and with it, the harvests end. With a feast already coming up, I think it wise to hold off for now."

"It would give us a chance to know each other more, Father," Prince Oliver said as he met Ezra's gaze. "Besides, I've been told she hasn't bled yet."

She cringed at the mention of it. She couldn't fathom the thought of having to bear his children one day. With this, she turned to face the king.

"Your Grace, a wedding this Spring would be beautiful, don't you agree? With the gardens flourishing as they do every year," Ezra pleaded.

"A Spring wedding it is then, my dear," The King said, sloshing back another drink.

Ezra breathed a heavy sigh of relief. Her only hope now was to concoct a plan to free her from this mess. At least now, she had bought herself some time, although she had no idea what she could do to get herself out of this abhorrent arrangement. She glanced around the room, staring at the red banners, the animals, and the trophies displayed along the walls. She wondered what her life here would look like if she were to wed her betrothed. Would she sit here silently fifteen years from now with her husband and children beside her just as The Queen was now?

She looked over at Queen Arabella and saw her eyebrows knitted together; her lips pulled into a taut line. It seemed The King was the only one who wanted this betrothal. Unfortunately, his was the sole opinion of relevance.

The large wooden door burst open with a clang, and another servant entered the room. He stopped several feet from the table and stood for a moment, breathing heavily as they all watched silently.

"Pardon the interruption, Your Grace. There's been an attack on one of the scouts, a Black Cloak. The people have set a fire in the square. The Blacks Cloaks are preparing their horses now to raid the area. They expect many casualties, Your Grace."

# 3

# Jarren

*Boom!*

Thunder roared in the distance, echoing off the mountains to the west. A flash of jagged streaks burst through the sky, illuminating his mother's terrified face in front of him.

"Hurry, hurry! Get inside your houses, and do not come out!" Rowan shouted, his voice struggling to rise above the chaos surrounding them.

*Thump thump...thump thump...thump thump.*

He saw the town hall rife with flames that climbed the wooden walls effortlessly. A large group of men stood over a bloodied body, his horse whinnying nearby. Jarren watched incredulously, frozen amidst the panic. The red banner that hung proudly on the building's wall floated down from above like an ember, flames tearing it apart.

He looked back at his mother and saw her mouth moving but couldn't hear her over the pulsing of his pounding heartbeat. She pushed him back toward the house, her eyebrows raised and her mouth repeating the same thing over and over again. He shook his head and looked around the streets, turning in circles endlessly. People ran frantically, elbowing and shoving people to push their way through the mass.

"I can't hide, Mother. I need to help these people," he yelled.

He yanked his arm out of his mother's grip and pushed past toward the town square. Horses' hooves swiftly pounded against the ground before him, and he saw a group of hooded riders entering the square. He surveyed the crowd of people in front of him. These people were all going to die, he thought. The Black Cloaks were merciless, vile, and less than human. He ran towards a young girl crouched down by the side of the fountain and pulled her up from the stone.

"Run! Get out of here," he demanded.

He turned back towards the fray, eyeing a group of children crying in the alleyway opposite him. He scanned his surroundings quickly, the busy square spilling down the narrow paths surrounding it. He saw The Black Cloaks slashing down anybody that crossed their path. Now was his only chance. He would be the hero, he thought, even if it meant having to die trying. He sprinted toward the children, avoiding the chaos as best he could.

He felt a body collide with his and was swiftly knocked over. His head slammed into the ground, muddy water engulfing his body. Screams and shouts erupted from the chaos around him, ringing constantly in her ears. Pain overtook him as feet trampled over his frozen body, stomping him further into the mud. He gasped, his lungs crushed and deprived of oxygen.

"Help!" he shrieked out into the muddled chorus. He closed his eyes and curled into a ball, wrapping his arms around his head. "Please," he sobbed, "Someone, please! Please help me."

Bodies trampled around him in a convoluted dance, the steps unfamiliar and foreign. A foot stepped into the puddle beside his face. Cold fingers wrapped around his arm and yanked him up from the ground, toppling him onto unsteady feet. His eyes shot open, squinting to see through his cloudy, tear-filled gaze.

"Go, Jarren! Get out of here; it's not safe!" Evelyn yelled, motioning towards their house. "Go now!"

He turned and ran, stumbling over running feet that were only trying to get to safety. Whimpering cries rose out over the panic. He stopped suddenly, his eyes searching the area around him. Shoulders bumped into him, and frantic bodies knocked him around. He turned and looked between a row of houses. In between two, a young group of children was huddled together, lost and forgotten in the pandemonium. He pushed his way to them and kneeled. His clothes were soaked through with muddy water, weighing him down to the ground.

"Come with me," he pleaded, "Please come; I can help you!"

Jarren offered them a small smile, tears still running down his face. The children stayed still, paralyzed in confusion and fear. Then, slowly, the oldest boy reached out his hand. He held it and pulled them up from the mud.

"This way," he said.

Jarren led them through the madness, trying to steer them from danger. A man fell a few feet from them, eyes open and blood running down his torso, an arrow protruding from his chest. He pushed them away from him and rushed through the door of their house, urging them not to look.

"We'll be safe here. I promise," he said as he locked the door behind them. His body was covered in bruises, numb from shock and exhaustion, and worry splayed across his face. "We're safe here." He slouched, his back resting against the door.

*Boom!*

"We're safe here," he mumbled.

He wasn't sure whether he was reassuring the children still, or himself. Either way, he no longer believed it. He sat with them, constantly muttering promises of safety and survival. He was grateful every time thunder rang out, covering the screams wafting in from outside.

"We're going to be okay."

Rain pulsed from the roof, mixing with the shrieks, creating a sound that promised to haunt them forever. The room reeked of mildew and blood, causing a wave of nausea, which was the last thing he needed.

*Crash!*

The window shattered, spraying glass onto the floor below. An unfamiliar body fell through the window, draped over in its place. Straight dark brown hair hung through the open frame, and red glass speared through her body. He gasped and pulled the children into him, covering their eyes and hugging them as they sobbed. A feeling of claustrophobia fell upon him, and the gray walls seemed to close in on him, no longer trying to keep people out but trapping them inside.

*Thump-thump. Thump-thump... Thump-thump.....*

He sat there with his eyes closed as tears streamed down his swollen face and never stopped whispering to the children. "Shhh...Shhh, we're safe here."

They sat in a pool of dirty water dripping off their clothes, shivering and rocking back and forth to stay warm. The blanket had soaked through and clung to their bodies, wrapping them in a cold, wet sheet. He couldn't think, couldn't move. His head was frozen solid. The rain continued pouring, lightning striking in the distance, for what felt like forever. Gradually, the noises outside died down one by one. Finally, he heard the door unlock and creak open, heavy footsteps approaching him. This was it, the inevitable moment he had been dreading.

*Thump-thump. Thump-*

"Jarren! Thank the gods you're alright!" Evelyn shouted. "You look dreadful."

He opened his eyes when he heard her voice and scanned her up and down. Her lip was busted open, and she was covered in blood, although he wasn't sure who it belonged to. An open gash stretched across her arm and cut deep into her skin. If he looked terrible, she looked much worse, he thought.

"I'm fine, don't worry about me," he replied calmly.

"Thank goodness!" she remarked, turning back to the children. "You're safe now; it's okay. Talk to the man outside, Rowan, and he'll help you find your parents."

He smiled meekly down at them as they scurried out of the building. He was convinced the last things they would have heard were his false promises.

"What happened to you, and how did you hurt your arm? You should've been here with me," he whispered, the sound of pattering feet still near.

"Rioters set the town square on fire and attacked one of the Black Cloaks. They came to capture the attackers and were met with violence. It seems they started slashing and firing arrows at anyone near the scene of the attack. I was helping get people and children out of the way when one of them nearly jumped on top of me. I tried to fight him off, but he was much larger than me. That's how I got the cut on my arm. Mr. Armitage saw me struggling and came to help. He gave me a chance to get away... He... he didn't make it," she choked.

Jarren walked over to his mother and smiled weakly at her. Lightning struck outside the open doorway and reflected off her face. He saw the terror in her dark brown eyes, her body still and unmoving.

"Soon, the Black Cloaks must have realized they were fighting a battle they couldn't win. Not tonight, at least. They gathered together and rode back to the city. They'll be back, though, with more troops, I'm afraid. Afterward, I stumbled my way back here. It seems the rain helped keep the fire from spreading too horribly, at least for now. Enough people here have died. We don't need any more tragedy tonight."

"Have you seen father?" he asked hesitantly.

"Not yet. I'm sure he's still out helping. He'll return soon, surely."

Just as quickly as it had started, he heard the chaos outside halt to a stop. He stood and slowly made his way outside. He looked out over the bodies lying there, unmoving, face down in the muddy pools of water. In the distance, flames danced across the sky, painting it with deep reds and bright oranges. The crisp, cold wind whipped across his numbed face, taunting him with every strike. He closed his eyes and inhaled deeply, suffocating in the surrounding blanket of thick, melancholy-filled air. His eyes shot open, and he stared at the bloody scene surrounding him; the realization of the night's events finally settled in his mind.

"The revolt... it's coming," he said.

# 4

# Jarren

"Evelyn is lucky to be alive. You should have stayed with her," Rowan said as he stood beside Jarren.

"I lost track of her; we were separated in the panic."

"Over two dozen people lay deceased before us, yet still, you excuse your behavior. You still fail to realize that this is not a game," Rowan said, staring straight ahead at the flames.

"I apologize... I'm very grateful to see you're uninjured. Mother and I were worried when you hadn't returned."

Rowan turned to look at him as he spoke, "I tracked the Black Cloaks back to the castle. They'll return soon with greater numbers; we must be off the roads by then."

Jarren hadn't quite understood the immediacy of it all before tonight. The revolt had always been an intangible concept. Something often discussed yet never yielding any results. He had witnessed his father plotting and planning every opportunity over the years. But he had never witnessed anything like this before. Violence was an everyday occurrence; yet it had always seemed one-sided. Jarren had never witnessed these acts against the Black Cloaks, not on this magnitude. It seemed as though his father was right. The people of Vaor were being pushed to their limits. The King and Queen's days of ruling were numbered.

They stood and watched the fire blazing, shooting sparks into the sky, swirling and dancing their way up to the moon. Faces from all around the fire wept, tears pouring down into the dirt below. He watched silently, scanning the faces surrounding him. He had been luckier than most; his family was still here. He stood patiently as the inferno slowly died down, and one by one, families returned to their houses to mourn together.

"The people have had enough," Jarren spoke softly. "Finally, they seem to believe that they, too, can have strength in numbers."

"All it takes are a few people brave enough to start change," Rowan replied.

"It seems those people have started to grow in number."

"Their efforts will be in vain if they continue these meaningless attacks. Coordination will be key to their downfall; rage on its own simply won't be enough," Rowan sighed. "We need to work together."

"Get up; you're going to be late!" Evelyn yelled.

He groaned and turned over on his bed, refusing to wake up. His body ached, his muscles screaming and sore. He half opened his eyes, squinting to see through the dim early morning sunlight soaking through the windows.

"Get up now!" she shouted, "We cannot afford for you to be late today."

She smacked the side of his head before turning and walking out the door. He sat up in his bed and watched as she yanked the garments off of the clothesline hanging outside and threw them into her woven basket. He couldn't remember the last time he had seen her sitting down. As soon as the ravens crowed in the morning, she was up and cleaning, baking, sewing, anything she could do to keep herself busy. He yawned slowly, inhaling deeply, and stretched his arms up to the sky. He walked over to the table on the other side of the small room and grabbed a piece of stale bread, nibbling on it as he tried to wake himself up.

"Hurry up and get yourself dressed."

After finishing his slice of bread, he changed his clothes and plodded outside, feeling heavy with every step. Last night's events replayed endlessly, forever tangled in his mind. His sleep had been filled with nightmares of the bodies in the dirt.

"I'm leaving for the day," he said as he passed by his aunt.

"Good, I'll see you tonight," she replied.

He dreaded the day ahead of him as he always did, wandering slowly towards the town bakery. The sun gradually rose as he walked, peeking out over the mess of tightly packed brown wooden houses. He inhaled deeply, the damp, heavy morning air making its way into his nose. He walked along the dark, empty streets, humming to pass the time. Jarren despised his job simply because it required him to get up even before the sun. He swung open the door, wincing at the blast of warm air that hit him as he entered.

"Good morning," Shea said as he turned to face him.

He wiped the glistening sweat off his brow, his face red and puffy from the hot air inside.

"Morning," he said dully.

He walked to the back of the stone building and began rebaking the bread to make biscuits in preparation for winter. He leaned against the counter and stared as the sky slowly grew bluer, birds chirping as they flew around on the back of the wind's gusts. He watched through the window as people descended the narrow streets as the sun shone brightly overhead. A group of girls grinned at him through the windows as they walked by, giggling and waving at him.

"Jarren, come to the front while I speak to the farmers about their barley," Shea shouted as he wiped his oily hands onto the front of his apron.

He walked to the front of the shop and grimaced at the line of people waiting eagerly in front of him. He had hoped for a slower day after last night's affairs.

"I'll take two loaves of rye bread," Jeanne said.

Jeanne was a friendly neighbor of his, and she came in once a week religiously for as long as he had been working there. She was short and frail, with wisps of curly gray hair falling all around her face. She smiled at him, wrinkle-covered dimples protruding from her hollow cheekbones.

"Alright, let me go grab them from the back. I'll just be a moment," he replied.

"Grab them from the back? Where is the other baker?" she asked squeakily.

"I'm the only one helping Shea nowadays. The craft guild has set the prices so low that he can't afford anyone else," he said as he stepped to the back of the room and grabbed the loaves.

"Oh dear, well, I know the famine must be hard on your business, but the prices have fed so many people who would've starved by now otherwise." Jeanne smiled at him and paid for the bread, "We're all grateful for that."

He worked his way through the never-ending line of customers until nightfall, when he was finally dismissed for the day, only to have to start all over again tomorrow. He strolled through the quiet streets, the puddles of water on the road shimmering with silver, illuminated by the moon shining down onto the bleak and lifeless town. The frosty air enveloped him, his breath cutting through it in a gray, cloudy mist. He shivered as he turned the corner, stepping inside The Rose. He pulled open the thick wooden door and was greeted by a wave of warm, stuffy air and the many people inside. He still had plenty of time for a drink, he thought.

"Hello Jarren, just the usual?" Thomas asked.

"What else would I be here for?" he replied with a grin as he walked over and sat at the stools in front of the counter.

The room was barely lit by soft candlelight and reeked of ale, crowded with people talking and drinking the night away. A disheveled man was passed out in a chair in the corner, as usual, an empty mug still hanging from his hand. Wooden logs lined the low ceiling, running across the width of the tavern. Tables were crammed together and scattered around the room, creating erratic and crooked walkways between them.

"Oh, I don't know, just to chat with your good friend Thomas," he replied cheekily.

He ran his clammy hands through his short black hair.

"Right, of course, that's why I'm here. And while I'm at it, how about a drink?" he smirked, "How have you been?"

"Business has been solid despite the hardships; I guess grief likes the company of ale," Thomas replied as he poured him a glass, "How's the bakery doing?"

He sipped the cold and bitter drink, feeling the liquid buzz down his throat, taking his time before responding.

"It's fine. Shea's let the others go; he can't afford to pay them. I fear my job will be next if the next harvest goes poorly."

"Well, I'm sorry to hear that. I hope it all goes well," Thomas replied.

He turned to serve the other customers who had plopped down beside him, greeting them politely. He sat silently, listening to the conversations around him, watching as people entered and left the tavern, smiling and talking amongst themselves. Even in times like these, a night at The Rose always seemed to cheer people up, he thought. Even as the ale buzzed through his body, his mind flashed back to the rioting.

He threw down a few coins and nodded to Thomas before leaving the dimly-lit tavern. He walked through the town square, past the charcoal gray buildings that now lay in ashes. Blood-covered stones circled around the fountain in the center of the square. He passed by the town hall, which now lay in ruins. These buildings had stood for decades, only to collapse in a matter of hours. Horses neighed in the distance, causing him to lengthen his stride considerably. He quickly darted through the winding streets and furthered his way to the city's outskirts.

Stars shone brightly overhead, illuminating his path through the narrow streets. A gentle lull overtook the city, blanketing it with its warm embrace. He paused briefly, staring into the stars above. He closed his eyes, letting the gentle wisps of wind whisk him away to a far-off land. One day, he would escape from all this, he promised himself. He and Ezra would find a way out of this monstrous place. Now more than ever, he yearned to open his eyes and be somewhere else entirely. He wished to forget this life, to be rid of it all. To forget the previous night's terror and the horror he knew was yet to come.

He opened his eyes and admired the wondrous world above him, tempting to take him away from it all. It seemed to Jarren that this was the world's way of apologizing for her wrongdoing, trying to make amends in the only way she knew how. One day, he promised.

# 5

# Ezra

She paced back and forth, her eyes never leaving the streets below. Flames rose out in the distance, illuminating the surrounding area with a fierce glow. News of the riot had brought their earlier dinner to a swift end. Usually, she would have welcomed the intrusion. However, tonight's news had been much less desirable. Thunder roared from above her, and lightning illuminated the sky. Her heart raced faster than the storm outside, chasing one another in a never-ending quest. She scraped at the pads of her fingertips restlessly, watching the birds swooping freely overhead. She wished she could fly away from this castle. Instead, she was stuck perching in the sky, watching helplessly at the pandemonium below. Of all the nights to be trapped inside, now was surely the worst. She blew out a heavy breath and sat at the windowsill, twirling her auburn hair in her fingers.

Even as the door behind her opened, she remained fixated on the sight below. She watched as a herd of horses entered the uproar. Mere specks from her perspective, she could only imagine their daunting presence from those around them. Jarren couldn't have been very far from the panic, she reasoned. He lived merely a few streets away.

"My lady, you shouldn't watch such unpleasantry," Marcella warned as she placed an armful of logs beside the crackling fireplace.

"What should you have me doing then? I'm locked away in this tower with nothing else to consume my evenings," she replied, remaining unmoved.

"Why don't you go and find Oliver? You both have a lot to talk about in regards to your upcoming nuptials, I'm sure."

"I suppose it could take my mind off such horrible things," Ezra replied as she stood from beside the window.

"He'll be glad to see you, my lady."

Ezra nodded with a small smile as she left the room. She turned down the stone corridor, listening to the sound of heavy rain pattering on the tower's roof. She slowly descended the stairway and crossed to the western side of the castle. She walked briskly through the great hall and spilled out into the frigid air in the courtyard. She quickened her pace and passed by the vegetable and herb garden before arriving at the throne room.

She passed through the doors and stared at the large throne perched atop a platform at the back of the room. Large golden feathers lined the back of the throne, standing taller than she was. Another example of their brazen wealth. She exited the room and passed through the banner-covered hallways until she reached the far end. The royal family's quarters were here, with the King and Queen's chambers at the top of the western tower. Lining the pathway were nooks inside the walls filled with stone statues of prior nobles and other kings and queens that had come before. She began climbing the stairs, pausing when she heard hushed voices accompanied by footsteps that were increasing in volume.

"The war can't go on forever," a male voice reassured.

"We cannot continue to fund these lavish festivities and support the army with our dwindling resources. The war must end if we are to do so," a female voice replied.

Ezra ducked behind a small statue, holding in her accelerating breath as she listened. Their lavish taste in ornamentation had finally become of use, she thought.

"It will end soon enough. Our army will arrive in Brunshire within a fortnight. Their victory will secure us the kingdom, and our troubles will end, I assure you."

She saw a red feathered cloak pass over the stone before her and peeked out from behind the statue. The Queen's dark hair withdrew from view as Ezra slowly rose from her hiding place.

"The last of the harvest will arrive after the feast and will satisfy us through the winter solstice. We will celebrate with the usual solstice celebrations, and then, with the end of the war, we will surely have a bountiful spring."

"Ah, spring," the Queen degraded, "the coming of our son's wedding."

"We agreed it was time he married. Their wedding will secure us the South. It's political, nothing more."

She stood silently as their voices drowned back into nothingness. It seemed to Ezra that she wasn't the only one who never envisioned their engagement. Oliver had no wish to marry her. It was merely his father's orders, the same as hers. She felt partially relieved by this thought. A purely political marriage would leave her more freedom to do as she pleased. It freed her from the expectation of love and romance. She would be expected to be present for the events, yet able to spend her time visiting the kingdom's other towns as well. Perhaps this arrangement could be beneficial for them both, she reasoned.

Ezra continued the ascent until she reached the platform halfway up the tower. She exhaled a sharp breath and knocked softly against the wooden door. She stood patiently and stared at the torch that hung beside the door. She watched as the flames danced, casting shadows upon the surrounding walls.

"My lady. I was not expecting you," Oliver said, "A lovely surprise, to be sure."

"Please, it's Ezra. We're engaged now; there's no need for such formalities," she replied as she stepped past him and through the doorway.

She was surprised to see that his simple chambers were not much different from hers. His was slightly larger, yet the opulence surrounding the castle had stopped at the door. She stood by the crackling fireplace and watched the raindrops slide down his window.

"I was quite surprised by the news. I'm certain you were as well," Oliver said as he closed the door behind him.

"We've grown up together, yet I hadn't ever thought of the possibility. We never spent much time together, I suppose."

He joined her beside the fireplace as he spoke, "I hope you'll allow me the chance to change that. I believe we'll grow quite fond of each other if given the proper chance."

"I hope so," she replied sheepishly.

"I would love to get to know you better. I would like to take you on a stroll through the gardens sometime, if you'll allow it."

"Of course," she said with a small smile.

He smiled, his brown eyes peering into hers. Ezra wondered if his pleasantries were sincere or merely for show. She had always found the royal family to be manipulative and self-serving. However, she hadn't encountered this side of Oliver before. Perhaps he was different from his mother and father. Perhaps he was decent, she thought.

She wandered back through the winding castle halls and finally made her way up the many stairs to her chambers in the eastern tower. She pondered on his motives, questioning the change she had recently seen in him. He had never shown interest in her prior to the announcement of their engagement. She supposed this could have been for any number of reasons that didn't require sinister ulterior motives. She spent the remainder of the night, her mind still heavy with doubt. She slowly drifted off into an uncomfortable sleep, dreaming of pain and suffering. She saw a vision of death swooping down upon her. Ezra thrashed awake, her body drenched and her breath ragged. This was the second time this month, she thought. She could no longer ignore this feeling growing inside her. Something awful was coming.

She stared out her window at the bustling city streets below. Evidence of the storm had washed away completely, leaving only the memory of the night's events. Days had passed since, leaving her mind tangled up in thought. The streets looked mostly unchanged, as if it had only been a horrible dream. She ached for this to be true, willing herself to make it so.

Ezra paced back and forth, glowering as she walked the monotonous path. She finally relented and slipped down into the castle crypts below. She carefully made her way through the unlit corridor and slipped out through the pathway. She passed through a narrow walkway at the far edge of the crypt and exited out into the outer ward. Here, she waited patiently until the nearby guard had turned his back to her. She quickly slipped through the gatehouse and ducked around the outer walls of the castle.

She walked silently past the guard tower at the entrance to the castle and shuffled her way out into the city streets below. She picked up her long red dress as she stepped over a remaining mud puddle, and stepped onto the cobblestone street in front of her. She took a deep breath and looked out at her surroundings, welcoming the sight.

She slowly walked through the winding streets before coming upon the remnants of the town square. The fountain poured water out of its stone mouth, and people walked the pathways around it. Across from it, the town hall sat in ashes, forgotten. She stared at the debris and the charcoal gray that burned the surrounding stone. Ezra quickly looked back at the path in front of her and continued down the streets, pausing only as she arrived at a bakery's front window. She smiled to herself as she saw Jarren, releasing a breath she was unaware of.

"Jarren," she said happily as she entered the building, "Thank the gods you're alright."

He looked up at her and smiled widely as he spoke, "I'm alright. We all are. My family, that is."

"I was afraid the worst had happened to you."

"Don't worry, you can't get rid of me that easily," he smirked.

She smiled and looked down at the stone floor in front of her.

"I'm glad. That night certainly was… eventful. I have some news, actually."

"Tell me later, alright? You shouldn't be here, Ezra," he said as he peered out the shop's window.

"What?"

"It's not safe for you to be here. Thank you for checking up on me. But, I can't have you getting spotted outside of the castle. Certainly not with me."

She stared at him, her eyes wide. "Oh… of course."

"I can meet you later. Come to the forest and wait for me up in the trees. I'll be done soon, I promise."

She met his eyes, her face expressionless. She nodded slightly and walked back out of the shop. She had spent days waiting ardently. It had never occurred to her that he hadn't done the same. Slowly, she made her way through the streets and over to the small grove on the edge of town. She walked to the edge of the wall and followed it down to the tree patch they had loved so much as children. She thought back to all the moments they had spent there, up in those trees. Those days were over, it seemed. They were in a different life now. They were different people. She was betrothed to another. She winced at the thought, afraid to acknowledge it as though if she did, it might reveal its validity.

She hooked her arms around the trunk of a tree and slowly reached her way up higher and higher into its branches. She settled on a flat branch halfway up the tree and awaited his arrival. She drifted back to the time she had spent here mere days prior. Her life had seemed so much simpler then. Before her engagement and his encounters with violence. It only exaggerated their different statuses in life, which had never seemed so opposing before. The ages of perching carelessly in these very trees were over. Sooner or later, those days would be a distant memory of another lifetime, she thought. Once she revealed her engagement, they would never be the same, she thought. This was their end.

# 6

# Jarren

Hooves pounded violently across the ground, neighing as people fled out of their way. A man in a black cloak stepped down from his horse in the middle of the square, searching the eyes of everyone around him. Jarren watched from his window, knowing that no good could possibly come from their presence. He scanned the man up and down, trying to see his face. A harsh scar covered the left side of his face, slashing deeply from his forehead down to his bearded jaw. His hooded head prevented Jarren from seeing any other of his features, creating a terrifying vagueness to the figure.

"In light of recent events, the King and Queen have implemented some new laws. Anyone found plotting against the King and Queen or suspected of treasonous behavior will be dealt with swiftly and without mercy. We have been instructed to undertake a more active role within Vaor. From now on mandatory curfews will be put in place, as well as random searches of any and all properties existing within these walls. The dumps you live in are no longer considered private and are now privy to searches without warning, authorized by the King himself. There will be severe punishments for anyone who is found unfaithful to the church or to our King and Queen. We will be conducting constant searches within city walls. No longer will we allow traitors and criminals to conspire in secret. We will restore order to Vaor no matter the cost," he spat.

His gravelly voice roared throughout the streets, accompanied by whispers of wind and ravens squawking overhead. He mounted his horse, and the group trotted back toward the castle, leaving a residue of fear and apprehension behind them.

Evelyn looked over at him, mouth agape and wide-eyed.

"It has officially begun. This is the beginning of the end," she said defeatedly.

"I need to go find Father," he replied worriedly, racing out the door.

Jarren ran through the winding roads and made his way to the south gate. He slowed to a walk and passed through the gatehouse, staring up at the portcullis as he passed through. He trudged down the stone stairs and arrived at the small path that led to the nearby forest.

The wind rustled the branches above him, clashing them into one another as he passed underneath. The woods enclosed him, wrapping him in a wooden cocoon. Branches protruded from the sides of the unkept road, sticking into the narrow path. He walked briskly along the road, bugs buzzing around him and birds dancing in the sky overhead. The path rolled into a steep slope as it cascaded down the mountainside. Soon, he came to a small clearing beside the path where he came to a halt.

A large tower rose from the edge of the meadow, white stone walls wrapped around the edges of the cliff side surrounding it. He made his way past the tree line and crossed into the opening.

"Father," Jarren called up towards the tower. "I need to speak with you. There's news from the Black Cloaks."

He heard his father's footsteps echo through the tower stairs as he descended, before arriving at the wooden door below. He watched as the entranceway creaked open, his father's blond hair appearing from behind it.

"Come," he said as he turned to make his way back upstairs.

They climbed the stone stairs up to the top of the watchtower. He made his way to the edge of the roof and looked out over the mountainside below. Jagged cliffs dropped directly in front of them, leaving only one entrance on the western side of the castle. He stared out at the water below, the sea waves rolling gently into the rocky shore. He watched as they slapped against the rocks below before turning to face his father.

"What's happened?" Rowan asked, his eyebrows knit together and his eyes piercing.

"A herald arrived in the town square today. He informed us of the King and Queen's new laws in response to the rioting. They'll be conducting random searches, and they're mandating town curfews. Mother's worried; everyone is panicking."

"Calm down, Jarren. I will call a meeting immediately," he replied.

"You can't! He said that if they suspect anyone of treason they will take immediate action. If the Black Cloaks find out what we've been planning, they'll surely kill us all," he said.

"It doesn't matter. If we have to live under their tyranny, we'll all be dead soon anyway," his father replied, his face expressionless.

He walked briskly through the treeline until he came upon the familiar grove. He spotted Ezra's fiery hair peeking through the leaves as he climbed his way up into the tree beside her.

"I really am glad you came to check on me," he said as he carefully sat on top of the branch closest to her.

"I thought you might have died."

He breathed in slowly, "I could have, but I didn't. I was careful."

"I was incredibly worried about you. That's why I came to visit. I didn't care about being seen. I needed to know that we were alright," she replied sharply, staring up at his bright brown eyes.

He studied her face, staring at the unfamiliar display of expression. Her long wine-colored dress was covered in a white fur shawl that she pulled closer to her shivering body. Her cheeks were flushed a deep pink that left him wondering whether the cold air was to blame or if it was provoked by something more primal.

"I'm glad you came. I've missed you these past few days. I remember when we spent every day together after you arrived here in Vaor. Now that we're older, we're distracted by obligation. Now, I realize just how much that time meant to me. If only we hadn't wasted all those days waiting for what was to come. Hadn't taken them for granted…"

She smiled, resting her head against the tree behind her, and gazed at the swirling clouds above. Once pure white, they now cast a gray gloom over the city. Even the clouds had been poisoned by the atrocities and evil that inhabited the city, he thought.

"We were children when we met, Jarren. We didn't know better. No one knows what they have until it's gone…" she said solemnly.

"I'd like to think you haven't gone completely from my life. Even if our visits grow less frequent. I'll always wait for you," he replied.

She let out a long breath before lowering her head to look at him. She gulped and rubbed her lips together, picking at her fingertips.

"Right," she whispered.

Jarren shifted on his branch, a long silence engulfing them. He stared as her eyes wavered, wondering what troubles lay behind them. An unsettling feeling resounded deep within him. He felt a sharp change in the atmosphere and hesitated before speaking, wondering if he would regret his statement to come.

"You said that you had news," he prompted.

"Yes," she huffed, taking a deep breath before she spoke. "It seems I'm engaged."

"Engaged?" he replied incredulously.

"Yes… To the Prince."

He stared in disbelief, his head swirling uncontrollably. Ezra continued to stare at him, her eyes unwavering. His heart thudded violently against his chest, his mouth unable to move. He had known this day would come eventually. All ladies of nobility were married off into other houses. Still, an ache resounded somewhere deep inside his chest.

"Prince Oliver?," he whimpered, "When is the wedding supposed to take place?"

"I'm not certain yet. It seems I still have some time before I'm to become a married woman."

"A princess," he paused. "You're to become his princess."

"A princess," she scoffed. "I never fit in with the royals before. I'm not sure how I'm supposed to play this part. I found out about the arrangement on the night of the riot. I wanted to tell you sooner, but I was locked inside the castle. I was finally able to sneak away this afternoon. I assure you this arrangement is purely political. Oliver and I have agreed, as well as my parents, before they left back to Rivers End."

He adjusted his position on the branch, fidgeting with his frigid fingertips. A sharp wind blew her auburn hair away from her somber face, causing him to pause. He tried to slow his breath, edged on by his racing heartbeat. Slowly, his breathing steadied, and a rigid calmness washed over his body. He stared at the ground below him, finding any excuse not to meet her wistful gaze.

"Oliver... You've dropped the titles and formalities already, I see. You must be spending quite some time together."

"We're engaged, Jarren. It wasn't my choice, but it's the reality of the situation. I want to get to know him, to try and ease the struggle for us all. I only want what's best," she pleaded.

"You think marrying him is what's best?" he asked, his eyes blaring into hers. "Ezra, you have never wanted this life. You resent the idea and always have."

"This is my duty. I have always known this day would come. I'm no more fond of this situation than you are, I assure you. However, I would be able to stay in Vaor. We would continue to be able to visit each other. If I were to be shipped away to some far-off place, that would no longer be possible. At least this way, we'll stay together," she reasoned.

"You will be queen one day, Ezra. Everyone in Vaor will know who you are and what you look like. The Black Cloaks will follow you everywhere, just as they do with the King and Queen now. You can't be seen sneaking off with the lowly peasantry," he spat.

"Jarren, don't say such things. My title was never a point of contention between us before," she said, her eyes glistening with tears.

His body remained rigid and cold, yet his insides were throbbing with grief. He wavered at the sight of her sullen face. He shook his head slightly, wishing it would rid himself of his tangled emotions.

"Before today, we were on the same side; wanted the same things. I always knew what you were. I knew that we lived different lives. You pretended to be the same as me, always saying that you never wanted a noble life and that you wanted freedom. And now you welcome that very life with open arms. Enjoy your castle and your feasts, my Princess," he grumbled.

He watched as a tear slid down her flushed cheeks, her face still and mournful. He dropped down to the frozen ground below him and disappeared into the treeline. His face twisted into a grimace, his eyes watering as he walked. She was no longer the same person he had grown up with, he thought. The Ezra he knew would never abandon her beliefs so quickly. She was surrendering to a life of comfort and aristocracy. The girl he had fallen so deeply in love with was gone.

"Now that the Black Cloaks will be keeping a watchful eye on us, we're going to have to be much more careful about where and when we meet, and who we converse with. The only way they will discover us is if they find us during a meeting, or rather the much more likely scenario that someone tells them about our existence. It is pertinent that we keep our plans to ourselves and avoid discussing any of this with anyone outside of this room. The random searches will add an extra challenge. I will be careful not to document any of our business, and those of you who can write would be wise to do the same. Lastly, do not under any circumstances be found roaming about late at night. If you are caught, you will be questioned, and that can lead to our discovery. Our only goal right now is to figure out our next move and try to stay hidden in the shadows. Do you all understand?"

Heads from all around the room nodded, looking uneasy at the news.

"Good, until next time," he said as everyone rose and began walking toward the door.

Jarren ducked his head down and marched out of the room, saying goodbye to Thomas and then walking into the sharp coldness of the air. He stomped his way home through the dark and empty streets, the night's events swirling through his head. He watched as his breath exited out, mixing harshly with the cold temperature. It swirled around in a white fog, the particles separating into the thin, damp surroundings. His body was frozen inside and out, his cheeks flushed a deep red and his fingers numb and lifeless. He clasped them together and rubbed them back and forth quickly, the friction slowly warming them up. Winter was here.

# 7

## Ezra

"Lord Percival of Ulster has graciously sent over a dozen of his champions to compete in the jousting tournament this afternoon. They will arrive with him shortly," King Henry pronounced.

"How long will my father and his clowns be staying with us?" the Queen replied.

"They will leave after the festivities have ended. A couple of days, perhaps."

Ezra stared down at her plate, prodding the venison her brother and father had killed before they left. She glanced up at the King and Queen, wishing it had been her family visiting instead. Ezra had only heard stories of Ulster, yet she imagined it was even more lavish than the castle here. She had encountered Lord Percival previously on several occasions. Queen Arabella was the striking image of her father with a strong bone structure and a cold and calculating presence.

"Are the festivities all in order?" Oliver asked.

"The jousting arena is set up for the tournament, and the Great Hall is being arranged as we speak. It shall be a night to remember."

"I look forward to it. Ezra," he began as he turned to face her. "It would be my honor to accompany you to the feast and subsequent festivities, if you'll allow me."

She smiled graciously at his offer. Oliver had always been kind to her. At least now, she might feel more welcome at the events, instead of her usual seclusion on the sidelines. Perhaps a partner would make these affairs more tolerable.

"I would be delighted, my Prince," she agreed.

The Queen smiled at the arrangement, nodding in approval at the Prince. Ezra wanted her time with the royal family to be as pleasant as possible. Once the engagement was announced, she would be required to keep up appearances with the Prince. Of all the royals, he was by far the most agreeable, she thought. She was glad that of all her possible matches, he was the one she would be marrying. Some of the other nobles she had met were much less agreeable. At least Oliver seemed genuine and kind, as far as she knew, she thought.

"It's settled then," the King said, taking a large swig of wine. "Lord Percival will be delighted by the news of your joining houses. We have always admired your father's control over the South. Now with the two of you set to be wed, the connection will be further secured. I foresee a strong future ahead of you, my dear."

She returned a small smile at the King's words. This marriage was, after all, wholly political, she reminded herself. Nothing more.


Horns blared above the roar of the crowd, signaling the start of the joust. The crowd cheered enthusiastically as the men swiftly charged toward each other. They held up their shields and lances in preparation, bounding to the halfway point of the track. The clang of metal rang through the arena, cheers erupting as one of the men was knocked from his horse, tumbling harshly to the ground below. The victor, clad in armor and his green surcoat, trotted proudly around the arena, boasting his skills in front of the mesmerized crowd. He took off his helmet, smiling a devilish grin at the women in the stands. Lord Percival nodded proudly at his champion, whom he had brought with him from Ulster. Ezra was certain that he had brought him to flaunt his superior skills over their own knights. The arena was decorated with blood-red flags hung all around, displaying their coat of arms proudly. The royals were all dressed in opulent gowns and their finest jewelry, dressed in colorful fabrics, and exhibiting their most extravagant hats. On top of it all, Henry and Arabella displayed their crowns proudly, reminding all of their superior status.

"I haven't been to a tourney of this size in years," Arabella commented.

"Now that you're set to wed, Lady Elizabeth and I would like to extend an invitation to our annual tournament and feast. We would very much enjoy your company if you can afford to make the journey," Lord Percival said with a pleased expression.

"We would be honored to join you come spring," Oliver replied.

"Then it's all settled," Lord Percival said with a grin.

Oliver turned and flashed Ezra a wide grin. She smiled politely back before turning her head quickly to observe the cause of the crowd's uproar.

They cheered as the remaining knights jousted until, at last, they declared Sir Quaran, the knight in blue, the champion of the tournament. They then all moved to the Great Hall for the extravagant evening feast.

Henry and Arabella sat at the high table on ornate chairs, covered in a canopy boasting their red banners for all to see. Beside them sat Oliver, Ezra, and Lord Percival. Long tables were arranged in rows along the hall, filled with a few dozen nobles, Sir Quaran, and numerous other esteemed guests. The wonderful smell of meats and ale wafted around the room, and the gentle candlelight mixed to create a warm and enticing environment. The hall echoed with loud laughter and chattering from the voices inside, accompanied by minstrels singing and playing harps and lutes for lively entertainment. Colorfully decorated jesters strutted throughout the room, emanating laughter from everyone who was near. Trumpets blared, signaling the next course to begin.

Platters of roasted wild boar were placed in front of them, steam still billowing from the blackened skin. She watched as King Henry stuffed his face with berries and chugged down countless goblets of wine. He laughed wildly, spitting wine on the table in front of him as the jester performed his famous skit mocking his people. Desserts were constantly served and flamboyantly decorated with animals. A garish statue made of sugar and pastries was made to look like a roaring beast, and pies were decorated with various colors and designs around it. Candied fruits were piled high in stacks resembling mountains, and wine was poured over the top of it to mimic a river rushing down the sides.

"Tonight," the priest said as he stood in front of the murmuring crowd. "Marks the end of the harvest season and the official arrival of the winter months. The full moon above us reminds us of the sacrifices we must make to appease the Raven. May he protect us through these coming months and gift us another year. Tonight I am reminded of the tale of The Fool King, which is stated as follows: Once, there lived a King and Queen who ruled beside a great mountain. The Queen was blessed with a child gifted to her by the Dove. On the day of the child's birth, the Queen died and was taken to live among the birds. The King was angered at the news of his beloved wife's passing and climbed to the top of the nearby mountain. There, he screamed at the Gods and blamed the Raven for her death. This angered the Raven, who had mercifully spared his newborn child. He swooped out of the sky, taking shape in his physical form. He snatched the King who had dishonored him off the mountaintop and threw him into the depths of hell.

This tale reminds us of the God's mercy and warns us of their justice. As we celebrate this holy day, do not forget the blessings we have received from the Gods. Do not be so foolish as to mock or dishonor them. Tonight we must all sacrifice and tithe to the Gods, and celebrate their blessings. Enjoy this night they have given us, for we never know when our last will be. Cheers to the Raven, and may he watch over us through the cold winter to come."

Everyone raised their glasses and toasted quickly before returning to the night's festivities. This was a tale she had heard countless times since she was a child. It was recited at nearly every celebration and had become a staple of the holy day festivities.

The feast continued long past sunset, with Queen Arabella and Lord Percival leaving long before the moon peaked in the sky. The King, Oliver, along with dozens of the nobles, stayed through most of the night, overindulging in worldly pleasures as she watched. Mummers costumed in elaborate outfits imitating birds and other animals performed a short play before impersonating figureheads upon request. They danced exotically in a wild fashion, crawling on the floor and jumping into the air, mimicking the animals they were dressed as. Later, a colored jelly made of pheasant was presented and placed on a pedestal in the middle of the high table, adorned by feathers with beaks and feet gilt.

The sound of laughing steadily rose with the moon, bellowing throughout the hall. They spilled ale all over the floor, and crumbs and scraps covered the tables they sat at. Ezra became overwhelmed by the musky stench that had progressively enveloped the room. Smells of meat, ale, and sweat mixed together in a nauseating flurry. As the night progressed, men became more and more drunk, singing raucous songs while hastily slugging down goblets of ale and wine. Their unpleasant chorus rang loudly as they stood arm in arm, singing at the top of their lungs.

"In the boozer
you're a loser
if the dice you're shaking.
You'll get hurt
and lose your shirt,
sit there cold and quaking.

Lady Luck, your gifts are bad,
you trick us, then you make us mad,
make us gamble, make us fight,
and sit out in the cold all night.

'Brrr!' The naked loser moans,

when he's cold and left alone,
shakes and shivers as he groans:
'I wish I could be
asleep under a tree
With a hot sunshine warming my bones.'

But now let's roll the dice again
and win some drinking money!
Who thinks about the winter's rain
while it's still warm and sunny?"

They sang and danced until they could no longer keep themselves upright. One by one the boisterous men left with women slung around their arms. They showered the couple with praises and admiration, stumbling over their words as their bodies wobbled and their heads spun. She winced with each proclamation, wishing that she was not on such display.

As the sky began to brighten with the sun's glow, the King was helped to his room, and carried off by his guards. Finally, Ezra was allowed to escape the overwhelming festivities.

"That was quite an event," Oliver said as he guided her back to her chambers.

"Yes, I hadn't expected so much attention. I suppose a royal engagement is rather large news," she shrugged.

"Ezra, I can't help but notice your disquieted appearance. I understand your hesitation to our arrangement. I admit, I too, was rather shocked at the idea," he paused. "My mother and father can be quite... overwhelming. I can only hope that over the coming months, you'll grow to care for me and to understand that I have no intention of mimicking their marriage and ways of life. I've grown rather wary of the people they surround themselves with. I'm afraid that many of them offer their admiration only out of pure obligation. I'm not oblivious to the faults of my parent's ways. I strive to become a greater leader for the people of Vaor. And it is my wish that you'll stand beside me when I become King."

She stopped and turned to face him. His eyes were shaky; his lips pulled into a firm line. She had never seen him so unguarded, so earnest and vulnerable. She stared into his sea-blue eyes, searching for an ounce of insincerity.

"Oliver... I must admit. I was apprehensive when I learned of our betrothal. However, I do not wish to spend my life pretending to be something I am not. I do not wish to stay locked inside this castle, watching as time passes through the tower windows."

"I do not want you to be unhappy, my lady. Quite the opposite, in fact. Therefore, I have a proposal. We have been placed into this arrangement by our parents, instead of by our own volition. We are to be wed this coming spring, leaving only a few months to prepare. I wish to spend this time together, exploring our potential, if you'll agree to it. I suspect that we could grow quite fond of each other if given the chance. In our time together, we have yet to quarrel over the many years we've known each other. Although our interactions have been brief, I have always found you to be a beautiful and respectable woman. All I ask is that you allow me the chance to romance you. I foresee the possibility that we could one-day rule side by side, content with our lives together."

Her heart froze in her chest, time standing still around her. She found herself lost deep within his eyes, wondering if his proposal was genuine. She formed a small smile, forcing her eyes away from his hopeful gaze. Her mind tangled at the thought of a romance with Oliver. She had never imagined spending her life with anyone other than Jarren. They had always been together, even if not romantically. Still, he was always by her side. The thought of Oliver replacing his position in her mind was overwhelming. She saw his face tighten at her hesitation.

"I only wish to make the best of the situation we find ourselves in. Although I can make no promises of affection, I assure you, I am willing to explore our relationship further," she said as she continued her way up the staircase.

"There is no doubt in my mind that we could build a happy life together. Already I know that we are well suited for one another. My father certainly could have selected much more dreadful matches for the both of us. I look forward to spending these next few months with you, my princess. Sleep well."

He bowed his head slightly before turning and making his way quickly down the stairs. Ezra stood silently, her mind turning their previous conversation over repeatedly. Perhaps her betrothal was not the atrocity she had first assumed it was. Of all her potential suitors Oliver wasn't such a horrible one. If only she could convince Jarren that he wasn't the monster he imagined him to be, she thought. She shook the thought of Jarren from her mind, refusing to remain bothered by his jealousy. It was her duty to stand by Oliver's side. He was her future now.

# 8

# Jarren

He pulled open the door and walked into the packed church, heading down one of the crowded side aisles to the Altar of the Raven. He knelt beside his mother before the statue, surrounded by dozens of others. A large pedestal stood in the middle of the altar, a large black raven perched on top of it. Two shining rubies were placed as eyes, peering down at the sinners below. He closed his eyes and listened as she began whispering The Raven's Prayer.

"Raven,
Winged one,
Forgive me for what I have done,
Lead me from my sinning ways
Accept my confession and my praise,
I call upon your wisdom; teach me to be free
Help me to see that which I cannot see,
Take me to the skies to fly beside you
To where all is good and true,
Guide me from sin and into truth
Breathe me full of life and youth,
My blood today I sacrifice
Take me to your paradise,

And free me from this evil world.”

Evelyn stood from the altar and stepped forward, grabbing the knife from the pedestal. She placed the iron against the flesh of her palm and sliced it sideways. She winced as deep red droplets drew from below her skin. She turned her hand over and squeezed her fingers, droplets falling into the red pool below. She set the knife back down and turned to walk to the other side of the church. Jarren followed closely behind her as they approached The Altar of the Dove and kneeled before it. In front of them stood a large fountain with a pool of water below. In the center stood a white dove holding an olive branch in its mouth. She tossed her gold pieces into the water below, swirling down gently onto a pile of toppling coins. Jarren knelt in front of the fountain, closing his eyes as his mother whispered The Dove's Prayer.

“Dove,
Winged One,
Forgive me for what I have done,
Lead me into better days
Accept my worship and my praise,
I call upon your charity, teach me to be free
Help me to see that which I cannot see,
Take me to the skies to fly beside you
To where all is good and true,
Bless me with riches and wealth
And keep my body in good health,
Accept my gift of charity
And give to me prosperity,
My coin today I sacrifice
Take me to your paradise,
And free me from this evil world.”

They rose from their kneeling position on the ground, bowing before they left. They walked briskly home, silence surrounding them.

When they finally arrived, Evelyn slathered her palm with honey, trying to heal her cut. Her palms were riddled with scars and nearly healed wounds from her many sacrifices. He scoffed at her belief that a few drops of blood could offer them protection from the evils of the world.

He watched as she grabbed the leftover pork meat and smeared it over their door, wiping the blood against the walls. This was an act he had seen her perform many times, and with each recurrence, he found it increasingly useless.

"That's not going to protect us, you know," Jarren said as he approached her.

"Hush, this is what they command of us," she said in a stern tone.

He scoffed as she looked at their door. Evelyn wiped the blood off of her hands and poured herself a drink as he lay down on his bed.

"It's just an old wives' tale. Wiping blood above our door will do nothing other than turn it red," he chuckled.

"It's a full moon tonight. Do I need to remind you of the scripture? Every house that wishes to remain free of death must sacrifice an animal to The Raven and smear blood above their doors. When The Raven flies overhead, he will see the blood and know that you have sacrificed to him-"

"He will spare us from death so long as we continue to confess our sins and sacrifice blood to him when he commands. I know. I'm familiar with the story," he groaned.

"It's not just a story. I will continue to do as they command no matter your opinion on the subject."

He grunted, closing his eyes and turning to face the wall. She blew out the candles around the house and made her way over to his room, pausing at the doorway.

"You're throwing money away to the church without reason," he said.

"I'm tithing as they command it. You would do well to do the same."

"It's a ploy to convince people to give what little they have. Nothing terrible will happen to you if you don't tithe to the church or keep your walls clean of blood."

"You've seen what happens to the people here. The riot was merely a few days ago. I'll do anything I can to provide protection over this household," Evelyn replied.

"That is the work of the King and Queen, not the gods. Nothing can protect us from the evil that lies within Vaor's walls."

"Even so, I will do what I can regardless of your thoughts on the matter. The last thing we need is the god's wrath upon us," she muttered, exiting the doorway.

"If there truly are gods up there, they abandoned us long ago," he replied, closing his eyes and slowly drifting off into a restless sleep.

"I spoke with your father, and I wanted you to know that I'm still planning on going tomorrow," Evelyn said as she sat down on the edge of his bed.

He looked up from the novel he was reading and stared into her dark brown eyes. He couldn't fathom what would cause her to volunteer for a trip to the castle. For the past few weeks, his father had begun sneaking into the castle to gather information. He deemed it necessary to listen and wait for the opportune moment to revolt. This was how he intended to find his moment. Jarren scoffed at the thought of it all. The people of Vaor spent their days fleeing from the Black Cloaks, not tantalizing them on their own grounds. This was a death sentence, he thought.

"I don't understand why it has to be you," he stated, setting down his book.

She sighed, "How can your father stand up there and ask the people in this city to risk their loved one's lives when he won't risk his own? It's wrong to ask that of someone which you wouldn't do yourself."

"I understand the politics of it all, I just wish it wasn't you," he replied simply.

"I know. I'm going to come home tonight, I promise you that. Merric is coming with me and if there's anyone who could guarantee my safety, it's him."

"He can't protect you from the Black Cloaks, you know that. I know you do," he stated.

"You're correct, he can't. But, we can do everything in our power to make sure that we return safely," she said as she stood from his bed, "I know you have a lot on your mind these days, but you should get some sleep. You'll need your strength for tomorrow. Be safe, Jarren"

"Promise me you'll be careful," he replied with a grim expression.

"I will. The Black Cloaks should be distracted enough by your actions. We'll make it."

His mouth pulled into a small smile as she walked out of his room. He closed his book and set it beside him, staring up at his cracked stone ceiling. Her promises of safety never consoled him. He knew how dangerous the task was. He knew that she had no control over whether or not she would be captured. Whenever they sent eyes behind the walls they knew there was a chance they would never return. This time, however, they had to. He needed her to prevail.

He stood motionless, crouched among the trees and shrubbery. His heart leaped in his chest as he waited impatiently. He teetered back and forth until finally the sound of hooves pattered along the roadway. When the carriage had arrived at the spot before him he watched as a dozen men leapt out from the treeline. He stood from his hiding place and ran toward the commotion. The two large horses pulling the carriage halted to a stop, thrashing their bodies away from the strangers who assaulted them. The men gripped the horses' reins and secured them in place as Jarren approached the wagon that was being pulled behind it. He restrained the horses and watched as the men pulled the people out of their carriage. His father ran beside him and began unloading the wagon's contents into nearby satchels. The men tied rope loosely around the passenger's hands and ankles and placed them on the side of the muddy dirt road.

The rest of the men made their way over to the wagon and began distributing the satchels filled to the brim with food. This was the last harvest of the season, brought up from the northern side of the kingdom on the other side of the mountain. They hurriedly unloaded the many vegetables and wheat off the wagon before disappearing back into the treeline. Then, just as suddenly as they had arrived, they vanished.

Jarren slung his sack behind him and raced through the forest, darting away as fast as he could. Branches collided with his body as he ran through them. His feet dragged in the heavy mud below him, covering the forest floor. He glanced over his shoulder and noticed that he and his father had been split up, separated in the chaos. His legs trudged on, refusing to surrender to his seemingly inevitable destiny. Sharp cries rang out from behind him. They had broken out of their bonds faster than he had anticipated they would. Soon the Black Cloaks would surround the area, searching for the bandits.

He slowed as he arrived at the edge of town and quickly made his way back to the safety of his house. He couldn't risk being seen running through the streets with a satchel overflowing with food. He calmly pushed open the door and slumped against it, pausing briefly as he tried to catch his breath. He exhaled sharply and made his way back to his room. He yanked the cover from off his bed and stuffed the sack beneath it, stuffing it down into the straw mattress to conceal it.

Jarren stood quickly from the floor as the door opened, turning to face the entrance. His father rushed through the passageway and unloaded the onions, cabbage, carrots, and other foods from the satchel.

"Were you able to hide it?" he questioned.

"Yes, Father."

"And were you seen?" Rowan asked, his wild eyes staring into his.

"No, I don't believe so."

"Good," he grumbled. "They shouldn't suspect us. Even if they raid our house we should be fine so long as they don't find your satchel. I've already burned all the papers that could link us with the rebellion. But, if they believe we have too much food, they'll kill us. They'll take any excuse they can these days."

Pounding hooves darted through the streets beside their house, racing towards the commotion. Rowan turned his head, watching as the cloaked figures galloped by.

"They're off," Jarren mumbled.

"It looks to be a lot of them. That should give Evelyn and Merric an opportunity to infiltrate the castle walls."

"Now we must sit and wait for her return," he replied, his face expressionless.

"She shouldn't be too long. The commotion will cause a panic and they'll be sure to discuss their plans. Once they arrive in the undercroft, they should be able to make their way up to the throne room. The Black Cloaks won't be patrolling the castle while they're out searching for us. With enough luck, they'll overhear the coming plots and be able to escape the premises quickly."

"And if luck isn't on our side?" Jarren questioned.

His father lifted his gaze to Jarren's eyes. His face was rigid and unmoving as he stared at him. He exhaled slowly, pausing briefly before responding.

"Then we pray."

# 9

# Ezra

Boxwood shrubs lined the walkway leading up to the fountain in the center of the garden. Beds were raised on either side of the path that housed an abundance of lilies, violets, and marigolds. Roses climbed on the trellis that wrapped the garden's arched walls. A large citrus tree stood at the eastern end, wrapped by a turf bench covered in chamomile. Ezra strolled past the flower beds and stopped at the north wall of the garden. Two large stone fountains were situated on either side of a large wooden door. She watched as a spout spilled water over a carving of birds. Carp circled around the bottom of the fountain, swimming endlessly. She reminisced as she observed their monotonous movements, forever moving and stuck within the stone walls that surrounded them. She couldn't help but fixate on their shared similarities. She too had spent her life circling these walls.

"You certainly make a beautiful addition to the garden. Although nothing here could compete with your beauty," a soft voice called out from behind her.

She turned and a small smile formed on her lips when she saw Oliver standing behind her. He smiled before glancing briefly down at the ground, a small lock of his brown hair falling in front of his amber eyes. He was dressed in simple black stockings and a deep-red tunic laced with gold embellishments. A fur cloak was draped over his shoulders offering protection from the sharp winds. He stood beside her, admiring the stone fountain and the pool below it.

"You flatter me," she grinned.

"I see you, too, came to admire the garden. It seems we haven't much time left here to enjoy it before winter stakes its claim. Although, the snow surrounding the trees and shrubbery always paints a lovely picture."

"Indeed. I find myself here almost every day. Such a shame that summer is coming to an end. The first snowfall should arrive here any day, and with it the end of such lovely blooms," she said with a small smile.

"Does the snow make you miss Rivers End?"

Ezra paused at the question. The winter there, although not a great distance apart from here, was starkly opposite. All year long the sun blazed in the sky, although the heat still settled around this time of year. Snow was something she hadn't seen until she came to the mountain-top city of Vaor. Winter only served as a reminder that this wasn't her home, she thought.

"I hadn't expected to be staying here for this coming winter. I had intended to leave with my family until the news of our engagement. I haven't returned home in years. I always find myself missing home when winter comes," she admitted.

"I'd like you to show it to me one day after we're wed."

She looked up at him with wide eyes. Her heart leaped at the thought of returning to Rivers End. She dreamt of the cobblestone streets that led through the winding town and up to the towering castle she had grown up in. It felt like a lifetime had passed since she had been there. Yet, if she closed her eyes she could still smell the salty ocean water spraying up from the rocky shores.

"My favorite place is by the river, upstream from where it spills out into the ocean. There's a shallow crossing where you can wade through the water and feel it try to pull you along. The sunlight reflects off of the water, shimmering a bright silver against the swirling tones of blue. It's enchanting," she said with a joyous grin.

"You must take me there. We'll go this summer when the water is warm and the flowers are in bloom. I've heard so many wonderful things about Rivers End, I reckon it's time I saw it for myself."

She basked in the happiness she felt while consumed by the warm memories of home. She met his gaze, her cheeks flushed from what she could only assume was the cold. After her father had demanded she stay in Vaor she had given up hope of returning to Rivers End. At least not for many years, she thought.

"I'd like that very much," Ezra beamed.

"I was wondering, my lady, if you had any interest in falconry? I would very much like for you to accompany me on my next hunt if it pleases you."

"I would be delighted to join you, although, I must admit I've never been before," she said coyly.

"I would be more than happy to teach you. We shall leave tomorrow then, at dawn."

"I look forward to it," she assured.

She watched as Oliver walked back through the stone archway and out into the courtyard. In only a matter of days, she had found herself living a completely different life than she had previously. It was all thanks to Oliver, she thought. Perhaps everything and everyone in the castle wasn't completely terrible, she thought. If only she had known what her life inside the castle could be like. Then, she might not have spent so much time wanting to leave it.

"We're set to leave tomorrow morning," Lord Percival began. "I intend on returning in a matter of months for the royal wedding."

"It would be our honor to host you here again, Father," Queen Arabella replied.

Ezra nibbled on the array of cheese and meat that covered the plate in front of her. She had always deemed supper a rather bleak affair and hardly devoted her attention to the conversations surrounding her. Yet suddenly, those discussions had become much more of interest to her. She peeked up at the man sitting opposite her and smiled at her betrothed.

"It will surely be the event of the year," King Henry replied with a chuckle. "I expect nothing less for my boy."

"Yes, we hope to convey a sense of… security to the many houses of this great kingdom. I cannot think of anything better to reassure our people that Vaor remains stronger than ever in these troubling times," the Queen finished as King Henry sloshed down another glass of wine.

"Well then, I look forward to this grandiose display," Lord Percival smirked.

Ezra had never wanted such an event. They were merely using her wedding as an excuse to flaunt their wealth, even if it was as dwindling as she had recently discovered. Flagrant displays of riches only caused unrest among the people of Vaor, she reflected. She knew better than anyone how the people responded to such things. It only angered them to see such prominent waste when they struggled for so little.

"I would be just as content with a simple ceremony, Your Grace," Ezra conceded.

"Nonsense!" the Queen hollered. "Your wedding is about much more than a simple ceremony. It is an event for the entire kingdom to celebrate. This is about much more than what you want, my dear. I understand you're not from around here and that you aren't used to the options we have here in the capital. You are far from Rivers End, Ezra. We are not commoners and we simply will not wed like commoners."

She forced a swallow and nodded politely in agreement, "Such lavish ceremonies are certainly new to me, I admit. I would be honored to be celebrated with such festivities. Your generosity is a blessing to us all."

The Queen's lips pulled into a smile that was evidently compulsory. Ezra sneered at her glaringly evident ulterior motives for such an exorbitant occasion. She expected nothing less from the nobles. Marriage for love was something feasible only for the commoners. She was destined from birth to be wed for purely advantageous purposes.

"I hope that you can adjust to our way of living here," she said palely. "I know that it's far different from your much simpler lives down south. It must be quite a change for you."

Ezra forced a smile as she stared down the Queen's threatening gaze. The thinly veiled ridicule had not gone unnoticed by her. Queen Arabella had always managed to lace her derision into conversation while maintaining an innocuous front. Ezra had grown accustomed to deciphering the many layers of subtext in these unassuming exchanges. She paused and watched as the Queen took a long sip of wine, never withdrawing her gaze.

"Actually, I've found it rather easy to adjust to such an… effortless lifestyle. In fact, the only struggle I've faced here has been adjusting to the rioting and civil unrest. I never imagined the capital to be so rife with criticism for its own rulers."

Ezra watched as Lord Percival, Oliver, and King Henry stirred silently, unsure of how to break the tension that cut through the air. Queen Arabella dropped her goblet onto the table, a small splash of wine cascading over the edges. The air between them buzzed violently with unease. She had much preferred the scantily hidden threats over the open antagonism that now surrounded her. Before another word could be said, the door that led to the courtyard burst open with a clang.

"Your Grace, please pardon the intrusion. There's been another incident in the city streets," the servant squeaked.

The King rose quickly from the table and followed the boy out into the bleak night. Queen Arabella glanced over at Ezra's face before silently arising and making her retreat. Ezra exhaled a sigh of reprieve from the hostile atmosphere that engulfed her only moments prior. She turned to Oliver, who offered a meek smile in return.

"I look forward to seeing you both again for the wedding," Lord Percival stammered as his frail body raced to catch up with his daughter.

Ezra slumped her head into the palm of her hands. Her lungs failed to expand and allow any minuscule amount of air to enter her body. She suffocated on the dread that overwhelmed her.

"I shouldn't have provoked her," Ezra mumbled.

"My mother has always had a gift for bringing out the worst in people, it seems," he replied softly. "It is by no fault of your own that the two of you find yourselves on opposing sides. She has been increasingly irritable since my father demanded our engagement."

"We still have months before our upcoming nuptials and already the most powerful woman in Vaor despises me."

Oliver moved to sit beside her and rested his hand on the small of her back. He pulled her hands from her face and peered into her now swollen eyes.

"I assure you, she doesn't. She has been extremely protective over me for as long as I can remember. Now, she is forced to share me with another. If it wasn't difficult enough already, she has to share me with the most beautiful, wise, and kind woman in the kingdom."

Ezra warmed at his words, her body relaxing slightly from its previous rigidity. She struggled at the thought of the Queen being jealous of her. Arabella had everything you could possibly want out of life, unlike herself, she reasoned. She couldn't imagine being of any substantive threat to the Queen. Still, she needed to be in greater control of herself if she wanted to win back her affections.

"Well then, I shall do whatever I must to help put her mind at ease. After all, I do not wish to steal you away all for myself," she said, her cheeks flushed a light pink.

"That's a shame. I think I would rather enjoy that," he grinned.


The crowd roared with excitement, deafening her with their raucous behavior. Ezra despised their fascination with public trials and executions. They were nothing more than tactics meant to scare the people into obedience, she thought. It was evident that royalty never seemed to mind how many lives were lost at the cost of their own entertainment.

"Welcome, dear guests," the Queen said. "In light of recent events my husband, King Henry, and I have reviewed laws and began enforcing new policies regarding high treason. We have devoted our efforts to capturing traitors and bringing justice down upon them. Our new laws have already begun making a difference and prevented traitors from parading around inside our walls. In front of you today stands a traitor who was captured by the Black Cloaks. They stand in front of you, guilty of treason and about to face the consequences of their actions. The punishment for high treason? Death."

# 10

# Ezra

She gazed out over the crowded throne room and climbed the stairs up to the side gallery. She shuffled between men and women of nobility adorned in garish cloaks and opulent jewels. It seemed as though everyone in Vaor had a taste for opulence that trickled down into every aspect of their lives, including their clothing. Ezra had never imagined a trial would be such a cheerful and lively event. Laughter rang out from around the stone room as warm chatter filled the air.

She finally arrived at the front of the platform and took her place beside the other ladies, knights, and other nobles of Vaor. She had never been required to attend such horrible events before. However, her newfound status had secured her obligation at all royal events, festivities, trials, and worst of all, executions.

She scanned the room and faced to find the King and Queen, along with the high priest, seated at the head of the room. Before them stood numerous cloaked figures clad in black. The Queen was dressed in a red and gold gown that spilled out onto the floor around her. She donned her red-feathered cloak, secured by large jeweled pins on each shoulder. Both the King and Queen were flaunting their crowns and the colors of their house. Although, his attire was much more practical compared to hers.

Two large stone thrones stood at the center of the platform with towering feathers carved into their backs. A large hearth burned fiercely beside her with large red banners displayed proudly upon it. Large hanging candelabras were strung up against the vaulted ceilings, the metal shaped to look like branches hanging above them. Soft candle-light illuminated the eager faces scattered on either side of the hall.

Loud shouts erupted from around the room as a man was guided down the pathway in the center of the room. Two cloaked figures dropped him at the steps of the raised platform. The Queen rose from her throne, a lull quickly overtaking the previous uproar.

"Lords and Ladies of Vaor... we stand before you today in the presence of the gods. May they reveal this man's guilt or innocence unto us. He stands accused of high treason against the Kingdom of Reina. May the Dove grant him mercy and the Raven decide his fate."

The man stood and turned to face the crowd, his face defeated and motionless. Ezra paused as she saw a quiver of emotion flash in his eyes. She had never seen someone so hopeless before. It occurred to her then that his fate had been decided long before his trial had begun.

"Numerous crimes were committed last night, many of which by the man who stands before you," the high priest began. "The last of the season's harvest was expected to arrive yesterday afternoon. Instead, the wagonload was attacked and looted by criminals hiding within the walls of Vaor. The Black Cloaks immediately rushed to the aid of the peasants who were violently attacked by these cowards. Fortunately, they were able to save the lives of the peasants and shortly thereafter, began searching the nearby area for the criminals who nearly took their lives.

On their return, an intruder was discovered attempting to infiltrate this very castle. After he committed incredible displays of violence against peasants merely serving their lords faithfully, he dared to try and breach these walls. He has betrayed his kingdom, his King and Queen, and his faith. He has marked himself unfaithful to the Gods and a traitor to our kingdom."

The crowd spat remarks of disgust and repulsion in a chorus of disapproval. Ezra quieted at their uproar, appalled at their willingness to sentence him to death so quickly. She gaped in disbelief at their vicious nature. Only moments ago they had presented themselves as the picture of dignity and grace. Now they appeared just as violent and lacking in empathy as a pack of lions surrounding its prey. If stripped of their titles and wealth, they would be even more vile than the most heinous criminals in the kingdom, she thought.

"Traitor!" the chorus rang out.

"Despite the Black Cloaks discovering him within the castle walls, he still maintains his innocence. In accordance with the law, he has been granted a trial," the priest announced.

The man at the bottom of the steps exhaled a heavy breath, his chest finally rising and falling. His eyes clouded and he let out a small whimper. Ezra gritted her teeth at the sight of him. She had slipped away throughout the castle's passageways countless times before. She hardly thought this action justified death. Still, his reaction to being granted a trial gave her a small sense of hope. Perhaps he would be able to prove his innocence of treason and be sentenced to a lesser crime, she hoped.

"However," the priest started, "As the Queen stated previously, the laws have changed. Trial by ordeal will be the singular option for matters of treason."

A harrowing sob escaped from the accused, followed by an encore of cheers from within the hall. No matter the outcome of the trial, he had been sentenced to death. She watched helplessly as he fell to the ground, his body shaking with each cry. She shut her eyes, willing herself to open them and be transported away from this horrid place.

"On the night of the full moon, he shall walk the castle's edge and take flight. We shall let the gods decide his fate. If he should crash to the ground below and perish, we shall know him to be guilty. If he is lifted by the gods and spared this gruesome fate, he shall be declared innocent."

She yearned to be back home in Rivers End; the people there would never celebrate the sentencing of a man with thunderous applause.

Ezra stirred back and forth, peering out her window as she had done countless nights before. She stared at the crescent in the sky, illuminating the empty streets below. Maybe this time would be different, she reasoned. She trudged over to her bed and timidly laid down, struggling to keep her swollen eyes open. She fought off a yawn, willing herself to sleep in peace. Finally, she sunk into a wary trance, her eyes admitting defeat.

*She glanced up and found herself sitting in a meadow, sunlight suspended around her. She relaxed slightly as the sound of splashing water rang from beneath her. She turned to examine her surroundings, to find only meadows as far as she could see. Birds squawked overhead, causing her to snap her eyes up to the sunlight that peered down above the lightly clouded sky. She stood, hoping to discover her surroundings. She ran towards the rhythmic melody of a waterfall nearby, hoping to discover its secrets. She ran and ran, never arriving anywhere. She placed her hands over her head and crouched down to the ground, hoping to stop the inevitable end she knew was coming. A harsh wind blew through the field, sweeping the light away with it.*

*She stumbled through the pitch-black walkway as rocks scraped against the pads of her feet. She blinked and imagined a streak of black sweeping past her. She stalled, her breath freezing in her lungs. A cold wrinkly palm darted out from the darkness, latching onto her wrist. She screamed, twisting herself free and turning to run from the creature. Her foot slid out from under her on the wet stone beneath her and she crashed to the ground. She scrambled onto her feet, turning in horror to sense the body behind her. The cavern had returned to darkness, leaving her trapped in its cold embrace. She sobbed and closed her eyes, unable to stop herself from picturing the sewn-shut eye that haunted her.*

*She opened her eyes to find herself once again trapped, surrounded by the rolling hills. Her breath turned ragged as she turned endlessly around the neverending grass. She screamed and ripped at her hair, throwing herself onto the hard ground below. She wailed, wishing herself to be rid of this prison. Suddenly, the cold hand grasped at her skin, tugging her down into the ground below. She thrashed, struggling to free herself from the woman's grip. Finally, she broke free and crashed onto her back, laying upon the very rolling hills she yearned to be rid of. She opened her eyes and found herself surrounded in a pool of blood. She looked up to find the full moon now staring down at her, burning branches blocking its view. She finally rested her eyes, a tear slowly creeping down her cheek. A wave of dread took over her, screaming ringing out in the distance.*

Ezra jolted awake, lurching forward and grabbing at the covers on her bed. Sweat fell from her brow, her breathing jagged and shallow. She stared at the pale morning light wafting through her window as her heart beat heavily against her chest. She stilled at the recognition of her surroundings. Already, the nightmare that consumed her was fading back, locked away somewhere deep inside her. She glanced down at her hands before running her fingers through her hair. Her wrist was free of marks, her hair free of blood. She studied the moments prior, willing herself to remember what had happened just moments ago. Her mind struggled to recall anything from her restless sleep. All she had ever remembered was the feeling of her frigid wrist and laying in a pool of red.

She slowly stood from her bed, walking over to the window, and returning to her previous position. She stared out the window before studying her own reflection. Her eyes looked cloudy and sunken in. She wondered whether she looked as miserable as she felt in that moment. She had been plagued by dreams for as long as she could remember. However, they had only escalated with time. It was as if Vaor was poisoning her mind, corrupting it with evil and misery.

"Ezra!" the door bolted open, Marcella's face coming into view with the soft moon's glow. "I heard screaming and I feared the worst."

Two Black Cloaks came barging in behind her, scanning the room before offering a small nod and leaving just as promptly as they had arrived. She stood from the windowsill, offering an apologetic smile.

"I hadn't meant to disturb your sleep, I apologize," Ezra said.

"Forgive the intrusion, my Lady," Marcella replied. "I did not mean to barge in on you."

"There is no apology necessary, Marcella. I've struggled lately to have a restful night.. My sleep has been full of nightmares. I forget them as soon as I wake, yet the feeling of terror never seems to leave me."

"I shall have herbs brought over from the apothecary. White poppy should help to aid your sleep," Marcella suggested.

Ezra nodded in reply, returning to sit at the window. She remained seated there each following night, staring in the same place. She watched as the moon rose and fell, and the skies darkened with each passing night. With each night, her dreams remained an enigma, shrouded in her thoughts. Still, she sat, convinced that one day, they would surely end.

"In front of you today stands a traitor who was captured by the Black Cloaks. He stands in front of you, guilty of treason and about to face the consequences of his actions. The punishment for high treason? Death," Queen Arabella began. "The Gods will decide his fate before us and reveal his guilt."

Ezra watched from the sidelines as the man was pushed up onto the tall stones around the outer walls of the castle. He turned to face the people, the full moon reflecting in his watery eyes. A sharp wind swept through her and she held her cloak closer to her body. He stood upon a few large stones that formed a pathway jutting out from the platform. The narrow pathway crumbled at the end before dropping downward to the shorelines hundreds of feet below. Three of the Black Cloaks lowered their spears, surrounding him. They pierced their weapons forward, forcing him to step further off of the ledge. They then slowly moved forward before repeating the action. She shut her eyes in horror and fixated on the sound of the waves crashing into the rocky cliff below.

"Please!" he begged. "I'm innocent! Please!"

Her eyes were locked on his, swollen and despondent. He took minuscule steps backward, tears streaming slowly down his forlorn face. Sobs escaped from his lips, his eyes wide with fear.

The priest bellowed, "May the Dove grant you mercy from the vengeful Raven's judgment, and may your guilt or innocence be revealed before us all tonight."

She glanced at the dozens of shadows beside her, all staring intently at the scene unfolding before them. Ezra's eyes shot up at the sound of the man's yells into the night's frigid air. Her breath stilled at the sight of the man being bitten by the spears before him, red gushing out from his leg. She choked as the man faded into the darkness, howling as he crashed to the sea below.

Cheers erupted from all around her at the man's disappearance. The chorus rang out into the night, carried on by the wind's whispers. Her stomach turned in knots at the thought of his wretched fate. She glanced up and met Oliver's eyes as he gazed at her from the front of the platform. She exhaled, her breath steaming in the frigid air around her. His lips formed a smile and he nodded at her. She stared back at him, expressionless, before turning back and disappearing into the cold night.

# 11

# Jarren

"Where is she?" he questioned, his voice shaky and uneven.

"She should have been back by now," Rowan muttered. "They must have gotten caught up."

"Caught up? They could have been captured. Or trapped somewhere in the castle. Maybe they need another distraction in order to escape."

"We cannot risk such a thing. The Black Cloaks are everywhere," he replied as he stood beside the window and peered out into the dark streets. "It would do us no good to get ourselves captured as well."

"I won't stand here and simply do nothing! We need to find her. We have to save her."

Jarren paced back and forth, his gait frantic and hurried. His breathing had escalated to a rapid rate, his lungs failing to keep up. His head spun, clouded, and panicked. Fury flowed through his veins, pulsing with each rapid heartbeat.

"Right now there is nothing we can do to help her. For now, we wait and strive not to get ourselves caught, too."

Jarren froze and stared at his father incredulously, "Caught, too? So you do believe that she's been caught."

"All I know is that they should have arrived long ago. I know nothing more than you do. But, I must prepare for the worst. The trips to get eyes behind the walls are dangerous and they always have been. I won't minimize that. However, she has Merric to protect her. He has done this numerous times over the past few years. I thought that would be enough to protect her. I still hope that I was right."

"You sent her into that castle despite knowing she could die. It's your fault if she does," Jarren spat.

His father whipped his head to look up at Jarren. His eyes were blazing and he exhaled a shaky breath. Jarren slowed to a still as he faced his father, waiting for his reaction. Rowan stared into his eyes, his body tense and his face pulled into a grim expression.

"I didn't think there would be any trouble," he answered hesitantly. "We've gotten in and out before without worry."

"You've said yourself how dangerous the Black Cloaks truly are. Then, you turn around and send your wife right to them. You sent her out there to die!"

"I didn't expect this was going to happen."

"You said we needed information. You said we needed to get inside the castle. You decided to send her. And now she's the one paying the price," Jarren spat.

"I would never have sent her if I thought this would happen, and you know that," he said.

"That's just it. You didn't think. And if she's not dead already because of it, she will be soon," Jarren replied, his eyes hazy and his speech wavering.

The door crashed open and Jarren turned his head, holding his breath as he waited to see the figure entering. He sighed, his eyes welling with tears at the sight of his mother.

"Evelyn! You're alright!" Rowan ran over to her and embraced her in a tight hug. "We thought you had been taken. What took you so long?"

She exhaled a shaky breath, her body shivering and her eyes still. She hesitated and stood silently as her frantically rising chest slowed to a calmer pace. Jarren stared incredulously, once relieved at the sight of her, he was now brimming with worry.

"Merric... he didn't make it," she whispered in a small sob. "He sacrificed himself for me."

"What happened?" Jarren questioned.

"I'm not sure. We... We slipped through the gatehouse and made our way up into the castle. We snuck through the undercroft and climbed up and out into the courtyard. We hid behind the well and listened as the Black Cloaks poured out from the stables. Then it was... dark and... quiet. The King and Queen finally walked out from the great hall and headed toward the throne room. We heard them arguing loudly, the Queen was furious at him. They were speaking of the revolt and the disloyalty of their people. She was suggesting it was his fault and that the best he could think of was a marriage proposal... I couldn't hear the rest of their conversation. We were too far away.

Merric rose from behind the well and began to follow them into the throne room. I hesitated, I wasn't sure that it was safe to follow them. He made it over to the door outside and ducked down behind a wood pile. He turned back at me and waved his hand, motioning for me to join him. I started to follow him. I truly did. I must have stalled somewhere in the middle of the courtyard. My legs simply wouldn't move anymore. It was as if they were warning me.

Then, I heard a shout call out from beside me. It was a young man, I think. I couldn't see him in the pale moonlight. He was screaming for the guards. I panicked and ran back toward the gatehouse. Merric was following me. He was. I could hear him following me down into the cellars.

We made it out of the undercroft and were coming upon the gatehouse when a guard came roaring down in front of us. We were stuck in the outer ward with nowhere to go. I was certain we were caught. I was sure we were both dead. Then Merric came from beside me and charged at the man. He stabbed him and threw him to the ground. I was petrified staring at him. He was bleeding and lying there, shouting for help. Merric grabbed me and yanked me forward to the gatehouse. We made it through when we heard many footsteps racing from behind us.

He stopped and let go of me. He was yelling at me to run. I couldn't leave him there. I turned to face him and that's when I saw a dozen men closing in on him. My eyes blurred and my chest was pounding so hard I could feel it in my head. Then I blinked and was running through the trees, darting away as fast as I could. Branches repeatedly sliced across my body. But, I refused to surrender to them so easily. I ran as fast as I could until I simply couldn't move any further. I fled behind a tree and slumped to the ground.

Tears welled in my eyes and I couldn't see anything in front of me. I sat there, breathing as quietly as I could, straining my ears to hear horses' hooves coming up behind me. But they never came. Slowly I made my way to the outer wall. I didn't know where I was, so I followed it down the mountain's edge. Eventually, I made it back to the outskirts of town and headed straight here. But Merric..."

Evelyn paused, her voice thick and her face frozen with terror. She began to sob and weep into her hands as Rowan held her. Jarren watched helplessly, aching at the sight of her.

"They have him, Rowan. I left him there and they took him," she sobbed.

"Shh. You had no choice. If you had stayed you would have been captured too."

"It was all my fault. I was worried and scared. If I had just followed him, he would be here with us now. I was a coward and he died for it," Evelyn whimpered.

"Merric knew the risk of sneaking into the castle and he volunteered to go with you. He wanted to protect you, Evelyn. He chose to stay behind and fight. He could have run, but he didn't. That was his choice, not yours."

"He only stayed to ensure my safety. They will kill him for what he's done. He will die on my behalf. We have to attack now," she pleaded. "We need to save him!"

"Merric chose to protect you. If we attack tonight we will all die tonight. His efforts to protect you will have been in vain. There is nothing we can do for him now, Evelyn."

She buried her face into his tear-soaked shirt, still whimpering and shaky. Jarren watched as his mother mourned before him. He had never seen her like this. She looked so vulnerable and human. Her many years of caring for him and running the household had painted her as a strong and rigid woman in his eyes. She was dutiful and a hard worker. She never complained or broke down. He then realized that he had never seen her cry before. She had always been a strong presence, yet, now she was frail and unsure.

Now more than ever he despised the Black Cloaks and their commanders. He hated the King and Queen and everyone who supported the dictators. They didn't deserve to rule, he thought. They had caused so much loss and suffering within these walls. Now, they had taken his strong and devoted mother from him.

He stared out the window at the looming castle that stood on the very top of the mountain. He imagined them sneering down at the world below them. They boasted their superiority every chance they were given. Banners with their sigil were hung all throughout Vaor. Feasts with a plethora of food were thrown for any excuse they could find. It seemed as though they only grew richer while everyone below them suffered. And he was certain they enjoyed it. That was exactly how they liked the people to be. They were untouchable with their army of Black Cloaks protecting them.

Then again, Jarren knew they wouldn't have their protection for much longer. A war was coming. One from within these city walls. The royals would finally fall and Vaor could be restored to its former glory. Then, they wouldn't be able to take away anything more from him. The people would no longer suffer as they watched happily. Their end was coming, he thought. This was only the beginning.

He watched the clouds roll past the crescent moon, lost in thought as he always was. He dreamt of the battle to come, imagining himself as one of the heroes from his books. He could picture himself on one of the horses the Black Cloaks rode, donned in something that wasn't tattered with holes. He imagined what it would be like to sit up there in the towers, feasting on as much food as he wanted.

His mind turned to Ezra, sitting alone up in her chambers. He wondered if she had heard about the events only a fortnight ago. Surely she had known about the traitor behind the walls. Yet, she hadn't bothered to visit him. Perhaps she didn't know, he reasoned. His mind darkened at the thought of another possibility. Perhaps she had fallen in love with Prince Oliver. She was probably sitting up there with the royals and sipping imported wine, feasting on boar or stew or whatever else they pleased. He sneered at the possibility of her becoming truly one of them. She had never wanted to be there before. Yet, Oliver had brought a change within her. Jarren could see it plainly.

Then again, she was one of them. She sat up there in her tower and looked down upon the people below. He had always seen her as something different, something special. Yet now he wasn't so certain. He dreamt of the countless nights they had spent together growing up in Vaor. It was a different time then, less fearful, he remembered. It was a time before the war. Before the Black Cloaks paraded the streets, warning all of their power. A time before they resorted to ruling with fear.

He thought back to the first time he had seen Ezra. She was wandering the streets, turning circles in the town square. He thought that she looked rather funny and approached her. She cried to him, telling him that she was lost. He offered her a smile and asked if she needed help. After talking for a while in the town square, he convinced her to let him lead her back home. Then, he had discovered who she truly was.

She returned many weeks later to thank him and had begun visiting regularly ever since. He was the kind boy who had saved her, and she, the princess from his novels. If only it had stayed as simple as in his books, he thought. Now, he worried he had lost her forever.

"Tonight is the full moon," Rowan began. "Merric will be executed at midnight. In light of recent events, I've called a meeting at The Rose to discuss our plans."

"You really aren't going to do anything to try and save him?" Jarren questioned.

His father exhaled a sigh and rose from his chair, circling around the small stone room. Light struggled to filter in through the small window beside him. The sky had begun to darken considerably as winter set in. The air would turn colder leaving many people dead, unable to keep themselves warm from the harsh winter. Rowan paced back and forth, fidgeting as he usually did. The unrest within Vaor had only intensified his panicky and frantic nature.

"As I said before, there is nothing I can do to help him now. He was dead as soon as the Black Cloaks got to him."

"He was dead as soon as you decided to send him into the castle with as much turmoil as there has been. You're lucky Mother didn't die, too," he spat.

Rowan turned sharply to look at him, his nostrils flaring and his eyes wild. His chest was rising rapidly as he slammed his hand onto the wooden table in front of him.

"I did what was necessary! We cannot win this war if we're fighting blind. We need to know the most opportune moment to attack. We're outnumbered and unprepared. Our people aren't fighters like the Black Cloaks are. We need an advantage over them if we have any chance of succeeding."

"You sent Merric into that castle and now you're leaving him there to die! Isn't that what this revolution is all about? Saving innocent lives? Yet you choose to do nothing about it."

"I'm not going to kill him! The Black Cloaks are! You seem to forget that they are the ones who are ending his life, not me."

"And yet you do nothing about it! You sit here speaking about the tragedy of his capture and how terrible it is. You are the leader of this rebellion. You are the only one who can do anything about it. You have the power to make sure this doesn't happen to another one of our people. You could end all the death. The suffering. The fear. You could end it all, but you don't," Jarren said, tears rolling down his cheeks. "You're the one who is too much of a coward to stand up and fight back. You're the one who lets his people get picked off one by one by the Black Cloaks. You, not me."

"Countless people would die if we attacked the castle."

"They'll die if we don't," Jarren said, staring into his father's eyes.

# 12

# Ezra

Ezra walked through the courtyard and passed under the stone arches into the garden. Snowflakes cascaded softly down around her, dancing as they swirled through the soft winds. She walked over the lightly frosted ground, the snow gently laying on the hedges surrounding the garden. The rose-covered trellises stood out among the garden, the deep red blooms shining brightly against the pale surroundings. She pulled her fur cloak closer to her body. Her long blue dress skimmed over the snow-covered ground as she walked.

Ezra thought of her home in River's End and how much she missed it. She loved the dewy glow that snow brought each winter, although it never ceased to make her feel as though she didn't belong here. She missed the white sand beaches, as opposed to the rocky shores of Vaor. The people back home dressed in much more flowy and light clothing than what was custom here. The people were much kinder and more informal, too. She simply felt as though she didn't belong here and wondered if she ever would.

Her mind turned to Oliver. She was set to wed him in a only matter of months. She had seen him last at the execution, smiling at her from the podium beside the rest of the royal family. She was perplexed at his unbothered demeanor during last night's events. He seemed unsympathetic, smiling at her during such a horrid event. Perhaps his suave demeanor had really been a front for a much more nefarious reality. She relived the night over and over again, unable to forget the sight of the man disappearing behind the castle walls. She shook her head as if it would rid her of the memory.

Ezra desired to know the prince's true character. She needed to know whether or not he could be trusted. She could feel herself beginning to fall for his courteous and charming ways. Before she had become too enraptured in him, she needed to know his true intentions. She needed to spend more time with him under the premise of romance in order to discover more about him, she decided.

She strode quickly back through the garden and out into the courtyard, beginning the walk to his chambers in the western tower. She crossed the snow-kissed paths and began making her way into the throne room, pausing when she heard a tense conversation pouring through the doorway. She hesitated outside the entryway, glancing around her to check for any onlookers who might question her eavesdropping.

"They said Brunshire was empty when they arrived. There was no army," a male voice squeaked.

"Brunshire is the capital, they wouldn't abandon their home needlessly, Henry," a female voice replied.

"We marched our army across the continent to attack Brunshire only for them to have left it. They rallied their army and left us stuck on the other side of the kingdom. I suspect they're marching here now. Our army is weeks away. If they have the head start on us that I suspect they do, they'll arrive long before we can intercept them!"

"Vaor sits atop a rocky mountainside. They will have the disadvantage during their assault-" she began.

"The terrain's advantages won't matter if we have no army to defend with. Without archers to launch down upon them and swordsmen to protect us we stand no chance of defeating them," the King spat.

"Their army is depleted and low in numbers. This is their last attempt to win this war. They must be starving and tired from their march. Surely with our unbridled position, we must stand a chance at triumphing over them."

"We simply do not have the men, Arabella!" he echoed. "I never should have listened to you. It was too much of a risk and now we shall pay the price for our foolishness."

"The Black Cloaks are skilled fighters. They can defeat at least a dozen men each. If we were to draft the peasants, any man of fighting age. We can win," the Queen assured.

"Perhaps, although we risk many of our skilled workers dying in the battle."

"If we are defeated they will kill us all," she replied. "The amount of laborers we possess won't matter if we're all dead. Besides, it wouldn't hurt if some of the men in the city died. If we are correct about the revolt we suspect will come, they are our greatest threat."

"Frankly, I don't see any other option. We could send word to your father in Ulster, however, I doubt his army could arrive in time," the King said.

"We shall send riders east of here. They can send word of the army's position and then we shall know how many days we have left to pre-pare," Queen Arabella replied. "In the meantime, we shall call upon the commoners. With the harvest season over, we can pull a great number without needing to leave many workers to tend the fields."

"The people won't be happy when they're told that they're being forced to fight."

"Tell them the army will take the city and kill everyone within the walls. The wives, children, everyone. Only a coward would refuse to fight for the safety of their family. If they should refuse to serve, they shall be executed," the Queen huffed. "That should motivate them plenty."

Ezra turned at the sound of a door clanging open behind her. She quickly opened the throne room's door and feigned surprise at the sight of the King and Queen.

"Pardon the intrusion, my King, my Queen. I only came to call upon Oliver," she deceived, her lips curling into a smile.

"No apologies necessary, young lady," the King replied. "I'm quite certain he'll welcome your visit."

She offered a small curtsy before scurrying down the center of the room and up to the chambers above. Silence filled the hall as she departed, a slight tension filling the air. She exhaled softly, glad to have avoided detection. She had clearly overheard a conversion meant to remain private. She gathered herself as she climbed the tower stairs, reflecting on the words she had overheard. The kingdom had been fighting a war for some time now, although it had always seemed so foreign. Although she knew of the battles, they had always occurred far from her. She struggled to grasp the thought of it finally cementing into actuality.

She rapped her knuckles on the wooden door, reminding herself of the pretense of this visit. She needed to return his admiration in order to lower his inhibitions. If she could get him to speak vulnerably, without worrying about her loyalty, she could see his true character.

"Ezra, I hadn't expected to see you. You must imagine my elation at the sight of you," Oliver said with a smile.

She returned his smile and looked at the ground sheepishly as she spoke, "The pleasure is all mine, my prince."

"To what do I owe the pleasure of your company?"

"I was hoping that you would escort me on a walk through the outer ward. It's been so long since I've strolled through the stables and been to the parish church."

"Of course, my lady."

Ezra smiled as he gazed blissfully at her. Oliver slipped into his cloak and donned his heavier boots before exiting beside her into the stairwell. They slowly descended the stairs, exchanging pleasantries as they went. She studied his every word, inquiring on the validity of his statements. She knew that his chivalrous ways were taught to him, perfected over the years. Yet, she couldn't stop her heart from swooning at his compliments. She had never been pursued by a man before. Jarren had doted on her before, yet never like this. He was much shyer, less sure of himself. Her eyes knit together at the thought of him. Jarren had been loyal to her since their first meeting. Yet now he seemed to resent her for her status. He had grown so hateful of the royals in Vaor that it seemed to seep into his opinion of her.

She crossed her arms, rubbing the sides to keep herself warm in the cold breeze. She scanned the courtyard, reflecting on the conversation she had overheard only moments ago. It only made sense that Jarren was on her mind, she reasoned. If the commoners were drafted she would be forced to fight. He could be killed. She shuddered at the thought. She couldn't bear to think of her life without him being a part of it.

"Ezra?" Oliver paused.

"Yes, sorry," she responded, finally turning to face him.

"Are you alright? You seem... distracted."

She softened at the concern in his eyes. Although she was uncertain of his integrity, she couldn't help herself from caring for him. Oliver was someone most women would fawn over. He was perfectly attractive and chivalrous, with a dimpled smile and honey-brown eyes. She felt horrible for mistrusting him on his parent's behalf. Yet, she needed to protect herself. Someone had to.

"I just miss my home. The snow always brings sorrow into my life."

"Ah," he replied. "I find some of the most beautiful things in life are laced with sorrow.  I believe it only makes them more sweet. Our joys wouldn't be so joyous if we knew nothing of grief. Don't you agree?"

"I suppose so," she smiled meekly.

"Still, it pains me to see you so distraught."

"Worry not. Soon we shall be married and I shall return to River's End. You'll find it to be truly beautiful, I'm certain. It's quite a magical place. Many legends were born from it. Nestled between the ocean and the river, surrounded almost wholly by water. It's a sight all should behold," Ezra said with a smile.

"One day, certainly, we'll travel south."

"I look forward to it," she replied as they exited the main gatehouse and made their way around the grounds.

After strolling the outer ward, she quickly excused herself to her chambers. She paced back and forth long into the night until finally, she was overcome with exhaustion. Her sleep was filled with visions of Jarren, a welcome break from the nightmares she was usually forced to endure. When she awoke, she was certain of her decision. She needed to sneak out once again, she reasoned. She needed to warn Jarren of the battle to come. She needed to protect him.

# 13

# Ezra

She slipped by the gatehouse, donning a dark blue dress and a black fur cloak. After evading the Black Cloak that manned the guard tower she shuffled through the streets. The cold winter air prickled at her pink nose and cheeks as she walked. Even as the air seeped inside her many layers of clothing she maintained a slow pace. She wanted to take full advantage of her time beyond the castle walls. Not even the frigid air could tempt her to go back inside. She zigzagged down through the winding roads and watched as the buildings grew smaller and the streets grew closer together. She walked by the chapel and paused as she came upon the town square. She stood among the ashes of the town hall. A merchant's guild had once occupied the very spot she was standing on. Now, it lay in ruins. She winced at the sight of blood still stuck in the stone cracks that lined the pathway. She stopped and stared at the fountain in the center of the square, admiring its stone intricacies.

She remembered all the days she had spent roaming Vaor's streets with Jarren. Ezra had never imagined herself missing this place. She wandered through the dark streets, dimly lit by the moon's glow. She stared up at the stars swirling above her, wishing to be among them. She imagined that all of life's troubles would seem quite small at such a distance.

Finally, she made her way back to Jarren's small stone house. He was luckier than most, she thought, as she surveyed the buildings surrounding her. Most of the commoners lived in cruck houses without so much as a proper door to keep the cold out.

She came to a stop and paused, staring up at the blood smeared above the door. Evelyn had always been a deeply religious person. She laughed at the thought of Jarren's immense disapproval. He had always thought religion to be a farce, or so he said. She had always found him to be brave for how outspoken he was, considering it was a crime to say such things. Then again, he had never been the type to follow every rule. His father was the leader of a rebellion, after all. Treason was the worst crime a person could commit according to the city. After that, breaking a few religious laws didn't seem so horrible.

She peeked through the cracked window, full of holes from what she could only assume was caused by the rioting. She peered into the back room and saw Jarren where he always was: sitting on his bed and reading a novel. Books were rather expensive so he only owned a few of them. That never seemed to stop him from rereading them, however. Most of all he loved the tales of knights from all over the world. He had always dreamed of living such a life. He had always wished he was born into royalty. If only he knew how horribly dreadful it could be, she thought.

She knocked gently on the wooden door, trying not to wake Rowan and Evelyn. She could only imagine the lecture the two of them would get if she were to wake his parents. Rowan had grown rather annoyed at their friendship throughout the years. Although, she never quite understood why. Life was to be enjoyed, she thought. Their lives were constantly riddled with awful things. Droughts, famine, sickness. The least they could do was make the most of their dreary and probably short lives.

"Ezra," Jarren said as he cracked open the door.

"Come with me," she replied. "Please... I must speak with you."

He hesitated, studying her eyes before nodding slightly. He stepped back into the darkness for a moment before returning with a heavier tunic and boots. His hot breath seeped out, clouding into the crisp air as he stepped outside. Ezra smiled briefly at the sight of him. Even after their quarrel she still had longed to see him every day since.

"Let's head over to the forest. If any scouts see us out at this hour we'll be stopped and questioned. Practically anything you do these days could get you into trouble, it seems."

She agreed, wondering if this was an appropriate segway into the troublesome discussion that she knew was coming. She hesitated, wishing to cherish this moment of peace she had with him. It seemed peace was something that was rarely afforded to them these days.

"I wish that I had come to see you sooner. I've been on rather strict orders ever since my father left back for River's End. The Black Cloaks certainly are good at tracking people," she said, offering him a small smile.

They strode along in silence for a while, passing through the buildings and out into the lightly wooded area. They stepped down off the stone path and onto the freshly snow-covered ground. She pulled her bonnet further down over her ears and hugged her cloak in close to her body. Her fiery red hair was tucked into braids that came over the top of each of her shoulders. She had always preferred this style to the extravagant updos in the north. They were much too prissy and took far too long to accomplish, she thought. She never could imagine why people would spend so much time on appearances only to do it all again later that week.

"I admit, it's been a rough couple of weeks without you. I couldn't stand how we left our last conversation. You know that I'll always care for you, Ezra. Don't you?" he asked shyly, staring down at the ground as they walked.

"I wasn't trying to hurt you, Jarren. I only wished to inform you of my engagement. I wouldn't have chosen this arrangement if I was given any say in the matter. However, Oliver isn't the man you think he is. As far as I can tell he is a decent and kind man. I, too, was wary of him. But, the more time I spend with him I find myself only confirming my suspicions. He truly is a good man, Jarren," she said with a sigh. "You know I would never marry if it were up to me. I have never wished to live this life. You've always known this. However… it's not my decision. I was born into this, Jarren. It is my duty to be married off to some lord, or in my case, prince. I must obey what my father commands of me."

"Why?" Jarren said as he came to a stop. "Who can stop us from leaving all of this?"

She stopped and whipped her head around to face him. His dark brown eyes were piercing into hers. She stared at him, searching for an ounce of hesitation. He was serious, she thought. He actually believed that it was possible to simply abandon their life here and start anew. If only it were as simple as that, she thought.

"Jarren, we have responsibilities here. Lives here. You have your mother and father to think about. You couldn't possibly leave them here in Vaor. Besides, I have River's End. I can't possibly expect to abandon my duty and ever be welcomed back home. We don't have the luxury of leaving."

"We could if you wanted to. Think about it, Ezra. We've talked about it ever since we were kids. We always dreamed of running away from here…"

"We were just children playing make-believe, Jarren! You can't seriously believe that I would abandon my life, my people! And for what? To run off to some tiny village somewhere with no money or work. You can't possibly believe that life would be better than what we have here."

"All I'm saying is that if you really wanted to be with me… you could," he said blankly.

He turned and continued his way into the forest. She huffed and trudged behind him, her face not feeling as cold as it had before. Suddenly, she found herself filled with heat at his unexpected outburst.

"Our lives are not that simple… Besides, there's a war going on. We could be captured by Brunshire's army. If they discovered who I was we would be killed, or worse, used for ransom. You know how awfully prisoners are treated."

Jarren exhaled sharply and slowly climbed up the tree in front of him. Ezra followed up the tree behind him before perching on the branch beside him.

"The war is practically over," he shrugged. "They've been on the run for the past few months and soon we'll have nothing to worry about."

"That's not true," Ezra said as she slowly looked up at him.

His face stilled at her remark, his eyes wide and his eyebrows knitted. "What do you mean? The war is all but won."

"It isn't," she said as she shook her head solemnly. "I overheard the King and Queen conversing. Our army arrived at Brunshire only to find it abandoned. They tricked us, Jarren. They're marching on Vaor as we speak. Soon, they'll arrive and our army will be stuck on the other side of the kingdom."

"That can't be true… We've been winning this war for months," he replied incredulously.

"We were. Not anymore. We have no one to defend this city with. We took the entirety of the remaining forces to seize Brunshire. Now we lay vulnerable, waiting to be slaughtered by their army."

His face paled and his eyes flickered back and forth. He muttered something inaudible as she sat silently, abating his response. Gentle snowflakes began to fall down all around them, softening the tension in the air. She scanned her surroundings and admired the dancing snowflakes falling before her. This was the calm before the storm, she thought.

His eyes stilled before slowly rolling up to meet her gaze. "What are we going to do?" he whispered.

"The King and Queen want the people to fight. However, I'm not so sure the people will want to fight for them. They want to rally them to join a cause. 'To protect their loved ones and defend their great city'," Ezra mocked.

"We're not soldiers. How can they expect us to win a war for them? Most of us have never wielded a weapon or worn armor before, let alone won a battle."

"Vaor sits atop a great mountain. The journey up will take days, leaving their army tired and hopefully weakened. Vaor hasn't fallen in a hundred years. The Black Cloaks are trained archers and will fire down upon the army as they approach. Hopefully, that should lessen their forces considerably. After that, it will be a bloodshed. All men of fighting age will have to wield whatever they can find to protect themselves."

"Men of all fighting age… You mean to tell me that my father and I will be forced to fight? To win their war for them while they sit up in their towers, feasting upon wine and cheese and whatever else they want!"

"Jarren, I-"

"How can they treat us so horribly and then expect us to defend them and their precious little castle? The people down here are starving and freezing to death. They know no such atrocities up there," he raged.

"Jarren! Please… What choice do we have?" she whimpered. "Would you have us open the gates and let them take the city?"

"Perhaps… Then we wouldn't have to die to ensure the King and Queen are able to keep stuffing their faces every night."

"They would kill us all anyways if they took the city! At least this way Vaor will still stand. You cannot overthrow the rulers if there is no city and no one to rule," she huffed.

He glared at her, his breath rapidly steaming out into the cold air around them. Her heart ached at the sight of the solemn expression displayed upon his face. Ezra had never seen him so hopeless and distraught before. He looked as though he had given up entirely, she thought.

"Enough people have died here already. Only a few weeks ago Merric joined the heap of bodies this city has claimed. When will it be enough? When will this wretched place ever be satisfied?" he cried.

"Merric? Was he the traitor?" Ezra questioned.

"He wasn't a traitor! He was a friend of my father's and a good man. My mother almost died beside him. He was good and loyal to the very end. He wasn't a traitor…"

"I apologize," she paused. "I witnessed his execution. I was there when he passed."

Jarren's face lit up and his nostrils flared at the mention of his death. "He didn't deserve to die. He was a better man than the King could ever be. The royals are just cowards hiding behind their walls and pretending they're better than us because of it. They are the ones who deserve to die. Not us. If anyone in Vaor is a traitor it's them. They have poisoned and corrupted this city for long enough. Now it should be their turn to die, not ours."

"Jarren…" she replied, her eyes wide in horror. "I'm one of them."

# 14

# Jarren

Jarren paced back and forth outside his house. He kicked at the snow covering the ground, watching as it mushed into the dirt. Ezra's words played over repeatedly in his mind. *I'm one of them.* She wasn't really one of them in his eyes, he thought. She had always been a lady, however, she had never been part of the royal family. She had never agreed with their views or way of life. If anything she was a prisoner being held inside the castle.

He inhaled a cold breath before finally creaking open the door and entering the small stone house. He made his way to his room in the back and stripped out of his layers. He threw them on the floor beside his bed stuffed with hay and sat, his elbows on his knees, holding his face in his hands.

Jarren had always hated the wintertime the most. His love of exploration and adventure always led to him climbing trees and running through the forest. He loved exploring all of Vaor's different cracks and crevasses, surveying every street he came upon. However, when the leaves turned and the sun began to hide he knew that his days of frolicking were coming to a close. He left for work at the bakery in the darkness only to return back home still in the dark.

He hated when his life consisted only of working at the bakery and lying at home. Most of all, he hated the lectures his father always gave him. Jarren never understood why his father was so strict and lifeless. He hoped that he would never mirror him when he was older. The thought petrified him, causing him to shiver.

He laid in his bed and stared up at the gray ceilings he had always looked upon. Years ago he had used a rock to scratch the surface, creating the impression of the stars in the sky. He loved getting lost in the constellations, dreaming he could be among them.

He sighed and closed his eyes, hoping that he could fall into a restful sleep. Instead, his night was spent worrying about the days to come. Although he was too humiliated to admit it, he was terrified at the thought of a battle. He had always envisioned himself as one of the knights from his novels. Now that he was faced with the opportunity, however, he was mortified. He wondered if they, too, had felt this way. He couldn't imagine Sir Frater the Great trembling with fear. Nor could he picture Sir Quaran quaking in his boots.

Jarren wasn't one of the knights from the novels he read. He wasn't brave or special in any way, he thought. He stood no chance of winning this fight. His mind turned to Ezra. He pictured her sitting alone in the castle, watching as the army approached. She certainly couldn't defend herself if the time came.

Perhaps this was why the King and Queen believed the people would fight. They knew that the people would never risk their lives to save the great city of Vaor. However, the people would certainly risk their lives to defend their loved ones. He would certainly protect Ezra, he thought. He would do anything for her.


"Father, I know what you're going to say. Please, let me finish talking before you respond," Jarren huffed as he sat down at the table beside his mother and father.

"What is it?" Rowan replied, his eyes glancing up at him from the stale bread he was picking at.

"Ezra came to visit me last night. She had news from the castle. Apparently, she overheard the King and Queen conversing about the war-"

"The war?" Rown interjected. "The war is over."

"It isnt!" Jarren squeaked. "Our army marched on Brunshire only to find it empty. Their army is marching here as we speak..."

Rowan and Evelyn stared back at him in silence. His father's eyebrows were knitted together and his hands stilled, no longer tearing at his bread. Evelyn's eyes were wide as she stared, her mouth slightly ajar.

"What does this mean?" she quarreled.

"It means that we all will have to fight alongside the Black Cloaks. All of the men and boys in Vaor will be forced to serve. I suspect they'll put us to death and mark us as traitors if we refuse."

"How are we certain she isn't making this all up?" Rowan questioned.

"You think she's lying?! She risked everything to warn me. To warn us. Ezra wouldn't do such a thing."

"Perhaps. However... It's something we need to consider. Besides, this could be the opportunity we've been looking for. The royals will be too distracted with the war to worry about a rebellion. Their attention will be divided. We can use that to our advantage," Rowan replied.

"No, we can't. If we attack the castle instead of the encroaching army we'll lose. Even if we are to take the castle we will immediately be conquered by the impending army. We're in the middle of a famine. They won't be taking prisoners. They will kill us all if they break through the city walls. We can't rule a city if there isn't anyone to rule."

His father paused and looked at him for a moment, his eyes unsteady. Jarren pulled his mouth into a taut line and stared down at him, refusing to be ignored. He knew that attacking would certainly get the entire city killed.

"What would you suggest?"

Jarren paused, wondering if he had ever been asked that before. "I say we fight. The Black Cloaks will launch their arrows down upon the army as they approach from down the mountainside. We'll use that to our advantage and hopefully they will be able to hold them off. At the very least many of the Black Cloaks will die. With any luck they will make up the majority of the casualties on our side. If they are to get through the city walls, we fight. We do everything we can to stop them from taking the castle. Then, once the battle is over, we attack. The Black Cloaks will be much weaker and the war will be won. Our army will dissolve as the men head home to their own houses."

"Its quite a risk," Rowan replied. "If they break through the walls and we surrender they might spare our lives. If we fight, we could all die trying to stop them."

"Yes, its a risk. However, I don't see us getting a chance to take back Vaor if they conquer us. Then, we will only be ruled by a different tyrant. We need to end it all. Isn't that worth the wait. Isn't it worth the risk?"

"Most of these men have never fought a day in their lives," Evelyn whimpered. "How are they supposed to win against an army?"

"If we don't fight we'll all die anyways. If we refuse, we die. If we surrender, we die. And if we fight, we may die. However, it's the best chance we've got."

"I've been waiting for an opportunity to come along for some time now. This is the first chance we've had in years," Rowan sighed. "I hate to let it slip by. However, I think you may be right. We can't risk losing what little we have. For now, we fight."


Jarren stared out at the crowd surrounding him. Wavering eyes watched all around the room, staring silently. The smell of ale wafted around the tavern and the dim candle light flickered upon each of their faces. Over three dozen men sat around the wooden tables at the back of The Rose. Every man in the rebellion had been called here to decide their plan. The fate of everyone in Vaor lied in these hands, Jarren thought.

"Alright men," Rowan replied. "You've heard the plans. You know the choice. This is the moment we have all been waiting for. The one we've sacrificed for. The one so many of us have died for. The Black Cloaks will be defending the walls leaving the castle vulnerable. This would be an opportune moment to attack. With only a small force we would be able to overwhelm the guards and secure the castle.

However, this would come at a great cost. The approaching army was said to outnumber the Black Cloaks considerably. Each guard would need to kill around a hundred men to defeat them. We all know this to be an impossible victory. If we were to storm the castle the army would likely make their way into the city and slaughter whoever lied in wait. We would leave our families unprotected. The people of Vaor would suffer and many would die. The army may potentially even breach the castle and kill us all.

There is however, another option. If we were to fight alongside the Black Cloaks and defend this city our chances of victory would increase greatly. Many of us are strong men and even some of us are fighters. We have been preparing for a battle for years, unlike the many people of Vaor. If we were to join them we might have a chance of stopping them. The Black Cloaks will man the city walls and likely suffer many casualties. They will be the first line of defense.

After breaching the city walls they will come through the gates and head up past the town square and towards the castle. If we were to focus our efforts at attacking the troops we might be able to stop them. If we attack the castle while its vulnerable we would be killing many of the men who would otherwise be fighting to protect the city. We would only be aiding the enemies. If they take the castle we shall only fall under another tyrant's rule.

However, if we fight alongside the Black Cloaks, we could win. We can use their casualties to our advantage. We wait for our army to return and for most of them to return to their houses. When the time comes, we will attack the castle like we have always intended to. The Black Cloaks will be lesser in numbers and this will create an opportunity for us to overthrow the King and Queen. We cannot let Vaor fall. Either a new dictator will take over and rule or we all shall die. Either way, the rebellion will end before it has even begun.

So, I say we fight. We are strong and capable men. We cannot let this army walk in and take everything that we have worked so hard for. Too many of us have sacrificed and died for our cause. We cannot let them die in vein. So I ask you to lay down your pride and fight beside the Black Cloaks. This… is our only chance."

Agreement rang out from all round the room causing Jarren to release a breath he wasn't aware he had been holding. His head sunk down to look at the wooden floor below him, stained from spilled ale and packed down with dirt from muddy boots. After years of suffering through his fathers dissaproval it seemed that he had finally gotten through to him. A small smile crossed his lips and he turned to exit The Rose. He slipped through the crowd and made his way out into the damp darkly-lit street.

Snow crashed down heavily upon him, causing him to withdraw into his cloak even further. He dashed through the streets, unaware of his destination. He finally stalled at the sight of the large tower peeking out over the pale red rooftops. He entered the chapel's garden, listening to the faint sound of water pouring out from the fountain. He walked through the narrow paths between the herbs and flowers that had since died off. Now only a few heartier plants and trees littered the once brimming garden. Slowly, he ascended the stairs that led up to the chapel doors. He cracked open the door, hesitating, before finally resolving and entering the building.

Jarren couldn't remember the last time he had came here on his own volition. He had been dragged here weekly by his mother ever since he was a child. He had never understood the need for religion before. He had always thought it foolish. Praying to someone or something as if they would hear you, much less answer your wishes. Now, he felt as though he understood, at least partially.

He passed by the altars that sat on each side of the path and walked between the row of columns on with side. He passed under the gallery and stared at the vault above. The ceiling was filled with arches and extravagant stonework. It seemed as though this was the only fanciful building outside of the castle gates.

He finally arrived at the largest alter at the end of the walkway. Here lay a statue of the Dove and the Raven, tangled around each other and grappling onto an olive branch. The legend of creation had been carved into the stonework, making it the jewel of the chapel. The legend had been implanted into the mind of every child in Vaor from the moment they were born.

*The Dove and the Raven had flown together for as long as time itself. After years roaming the skies they decided they needed somewhere to land, something to look down upon. So, they created the world. In this way they could rest and admire what they had created together. They first created the olive tree, which rooted itself into the ground. Life spread from the tree and an entire world blossomed out of it. However, after the world was created they needed to create things to live upon it. The merciful Dove decided to create people to enjoy the world. The Raven allowed the people to live in the world that they had created, so long as they devoted their lives to worshiping the gods that had given them life. The duty of the people is to continue tithing and appeasing the gods in order to maintain this peace. So long as we are faithful to the gods, we shall continue to receive their blessings. However, if we are to disobey, we shall suffer. The Raven is not so merciful as the Dove. If we should forsake them, men shall die and famines shall rule the world. Great floods and fires will cover the land. The Raven demands that we remain faithful as a sign of our gratitude for this gift of life. You must always remember this and continue to keep faith.*

Jarren had been given this sermon every year, although he always deemed it propaganda, casting fear into those who heard it. He believed it was merely a tactic to prevent the people from uprising. Up until now… it had worked.

Jarren knelt down before the altar and stared at the flickering flames from the candles lit in front of it. A ring of flames encircled the stone base, the small streams of smoke stretching to the arched ceiling above. Above the candles stood a circle of incense, waiting to be lit.

Jarren released a breath and picked up one of the candles, holding it to the stick of herbs. He watched as it lit before lowering the candle back to its resting place. He gently blew the flame out and watched as the incense released a thick fragrant smoke that billowed to the sky above. The air smelled of frankincense as he hovered above the incense. He asked for protection from the Raven and mercy from the Dove. He willed them to spare him, to watch over his mother and father, Ezra, and even himself. He had never believed in them before. Yet, he felt as though he had no choice other than to turn to them now. Jarren still possessed no confidence that this would work. However, he had to try.

Maybe this would save them.

# 15

## Ezra

She pulled out the back of the chair, its wooden legs creaking over the stone floor beneath her. The sound filled the room, breaking the silence that had previously overwhelmed it. Erza sat at the far end of the table across from Oliver, just as they had done each night prior. However, this night starkly contrasted all that had come before. They all took large gulps of their wine and picked at the food in front of them. It seemed as though Ezra wasn't the only one who was far too enraptured in thought to worry about something as impertinent at eating. The thought alone of eating at a time such as this was nauseating.

"Ezra," Oliver said as he cleared his throat. "I was hoping to have one last visit with you this evening. I would like to walk the castle grounds with you, if it pleases you."

"The pleasure is all mine," she responded, unable to deny him his potentially last wish.

"Well, I'm sure we will all be eating here together again tomorrow evening. Nothing to worry about," the King said as he stood from his chair.

King Henry sloshed down the hall and into his chambers, followed by a scurry of servants as he tripped his way up the stairs. Queen Arabella huffed as he left, sipping slowly on her wine as she stared Ezra up and down.

"I hope to see you in the throne room tomorrow, Ezra. All the ladies of the castle go there during battle. Although, I've never had to wait there myself. Never had the need."

"Of course my Queen, I will be there."

The Queen offered a polite smile before slithering out of her seat and excusing herself from the room. Ezra turned to look up at Oliver and met his amber gaze. He looked… almost worried, she thought. He had always seemed suave and brave, leading her to never imagine that he was capable of feeling such an emotion.

"How are you feeling in regards to the battle tomorrow?" Ezra asked timidly.

"I will do anything for you, Ezra. I would gladly die to protect you. Now is merely a chance to prove it," he said with a small smirk that didn't reach his eyes.

"I'm frightened. I've never been anywhere near a battle before. And you, you're going out to fight?" Ezra cried.

"It's my duty, Ezra. I won't abandon my people now. Someday this castle will be ours. The people out there will remember who fought for them. I will be one of them," he said simply.

"What if something happens to you?" Ezra mewled. "What will you do if you get hurt?"

"I am an excellent fighter, Ezra. Now I can finally prove it on the field. I finally get to put all my years of training into use. Trust me… I will be just fine. I won't let anything happen to you. I promise."

"Don't make promises you can't keep."

"Shhh…" he soothed. "We're going to be just fine."

"You are severely outnumbered. You are surrounded by civilians and facing an army," she pleaded.

"Their soldiers have been fighting for months. This is a final attempt to win by taking our castle. They know that they would be defeated if they met our army in battle. They are tired and hungry and we will pick them off one by one as they climb up the mountainside. I promise."

"What if you die, Oliver?" she questioned. "Then what am I sup-posed to do?"

He stood from his seat and crossed over to the one beside her. He lowered his head to meet her eyeline and placed his hand under her chin. "Ezra, don't worry about me. Just the thought of you up in the castle could make me defeat that entire army for you."

"I don't belong here, Oliver. Certainly not without you here."

She couldn't fathom the thought of being stuck in the castle with a grieving King and Queen. They were already miserable enough as is. The King would only further drown himself in ale and wine. The Queen would grow more intolerable and vile, if possible. Living in Vaor had always been hard. But, she couldn't bear the thought of living here without the ability to visit Jarren and without so much as a friend in the castle.

"We will rule together one day, Ezra. I promise."

A small smile crept over her face as he kissed her hand. He rose from his chair and smiled, giving her a brief nod before holding his arm out for her. Ezra stood and slipped her arm through his, holding it against her. They made their way out into the crisp air and walked over to the balcony. Only a few fortnights ago this had been the sight of a nightmare she yearned to forget. Now all she could stare at was the moon's soft glow reflecting off the black water. She looked out upon the sea and watched the waves crash against the stone cliffs below. Snow covered the rocky shoreline, ice forming all over the ground surrounding it. Ezra inhaled the fresh scent of salty water stuffing the air. She wrinkled her nose as the cold wind whipped across her face.

"What a waste of a perfectly lovely night," Oliver sighed.

"Just for a moment... I don't want to talk about what's to come. I want to forget about it. Forget about everything."

"If only we could exhale our troubles away."

"I wish that life were as simple as that," Ezra said softly. "I wish that I didn't have these troubles. Of all the years I've spent here, I've never wanted to leave this city so badly. Take everything I own and everyone that I love and leave this place behind me."

Ezra turned and began strolling along the wall that surrounded the castle. She wandered over to the section of the wall that sat beside her chamber walls. She looked down upon the river of brown roofs, wrapped by stone towers and walls. Ezra sighed at the thought of never seeing it again. Jarren was right... You never admire what you have until someone threatens to take it all away from you.

"One day you will grow to love Vaor just as you will grow to love me. This is your duty, just as I have mine. Vaor is our home. We must do what we can to protect it."

Ezra turned to examine his face as he stared out over the city. The only light sources she could see were coming from the chapel. She couldn't imagine how many people had lit candles and incense to pray to the gods. She wondered if the billowing smoke could reach this high, let alone make its way all the way up to them.

Ezra wondered whether he would have treated any lady he had been matched with any differently than he treated her. When speaking of the events to follow he had never admitted to any worry or genuine emotion. She couldn't decide whether it was out of a need to be seen as brave and chivalrous, or simply because he couldn't be vulnerable with her. Either way, she decided that she preferred honesty. Jarren had never treated her this way.

Her mind spun at the thought of Jarren out on the battlefield tomorrow. He would be petrified to encounter real combat. This was life or death, nothing like he had seen before. He had dealt with many horrible people in Vaor, yet he had never staked his life on it. The Black Cloaks had always kept tight control over the city. The crime was almost completely theft and other such annoyances. No one would commit more heinous acts in fear of execution.

Yet, Jarren would have admitted his doubts and worries to her. She deemed that to be a much higher form of bravery than whatever kind Oliver possessed. The air in her lungs failed to satisfy her needs. She felt as though she was standing there suffocating out in the frigid air. A man she loved was going out into battle and there was nothing she could do to protect him.

*Crash!*

The first echo of battle clanged throughout the city's walls. Ezra shuddered at the eruption of sound within the castle. She glanced down at the wooden table before her and wrapped her hand along the edge, trying to brace herself and steady her woozy head. She sat beside the other ladies of the castle, stuffed into the back corner of the throne room. This was the furthest point from the main gate that led to the front castle. At least they didn't need to worry about defending from all sides of the city, Ezra thought. They were backed up against the edge of the mountain, a steep drop-off stood only a few feet from the wall they had braced themselves upon.

*Boom!*

Ezra winced. That must have been the city's walls. The army had breached through the main gate, she thought. It would only be a matter of time before the castle was raided and they were all killed.

She stared up at the arched stone ceiling and her mind drifted to Jarren. He didn't have the luxury of strong stone walls protecting him. She tried to imagine what he was doing and how he was feeling. Was he trembling as he watched them pour into the city? Was he in the midst of battle? Was it something much more sinister?

*Thud!*

"Jarren," she wept silently.

"Ladies, please. Have faith in the Black Cloaks. Have faith in the people of Vaor and their willingness to sacrifice their lives for yours. They will do whatever they must to protect us. You should not fear death. We will not face it today," the Queen preached.

A few faint whimpers rang out from the women and girls that sat around her. She sipped at the wine in her goblet, swirling it around as she stared at it. At least they had tried to make the women comfortable. She couldn't imagine that the wine and platters of fruit and cheese could ease the dread and ache that consumed her. However, it couldn't hurt to try the wine, she reasoned. She took another swig, her head clouded with wine and thoughts of Jarren.

"You look worried, my lady. Don't worry. He will be alright," Marcella said as she took a seat beside her.

"How can you be so sure?" Ezra asked, her eyes glassy.

"Oliver has been training for many years. He's an excellent fighter. He will protect us, Ezra."

"Right… of course," she stammered with a small nod.

# 16

# Jarren

*Ding ding, Ding ding.*

The bells echoed throughout Vaor, signaling the beginning of the invasion. The army was approaching the city's walls. This moment had finally arrived; the one Jarren had been dreading for days.

I can do this, he repeated silently. I can do this. I can do this… His feet planted themselves in place and his wide eyes remained trained on the wall. Jarren dreaded what was to come. As much as he wished that he was brave like the heroes from his novels were, his body refused to cooperate. His feet grew roots in the soil as he stood, forever stuck to that very spot.

Rowan crossed the few steps to face him, looking into his eyes as he spoke, "You're going to be fine. We need to fight. We can't simply wait here for the moment to pass."

"Why not?" he asked worriedly.

Rowan sighed, "It will take everyone to win the war. I know that you're scared to die. But, everyone here is scared, too. Every one of the people defending the walls right now. Everyone is risking their lives for their neighbors, friends, and strangers. They are all we have to help us. How would you feel if you let them take on this fight alone? You need to defend this city. If the army breaks through they will reach the castle. They will reach Ezra. We cannot start to fall apart now. We either all attack, or none of us do. And we will die if we don't attack," he reasoned, urgency thick in his voice.

He sniffled. "I know. I'm just terrified."

Rowan smiled meekly and pulled his tense body into a tight hug. Rowan slowly stepped backward, forcing his feet to unplant themselves from the ground. Jarren walked silently as he led him closer, his mind teetering on the edge of stability. His breathing became ragged as he approached the gray separator, hiding in the shrubbery as they positioned themselves around the gate.

A cacophony of footsteps roared as they grew in volume, quickly approaching the city walls. Chants, yells, and battle cries soared over the sounds, engulfing Vaor in their animalistic screams. This was the last sound he would hear, Jarren worried.

He waited in the cover of the closely grown trees as he pulled out the dagger Rowan had given him. As much as he had opposed receiving the weapon when he had handed it to him for protection, he was now thankful that he had it. His mind flashed back to the sight of bodies covered with stab wounds and arrows. He remembered the bodies that littered the town square. He despised the Black Cloaks for what they had done to those people. He never thought that he would be on the same side as the killers.

His breath hitched in his throat as Rowan and the others waited with bated breaths. Shouting erupted from the top of the wall, followed by heavy thuds that were sliced through with silence. Time froze as his head raced endlessly with panic and dread, his limbs going numb from the apprehension.

"Draw... Nock... Loose!" a man called out from the walls.

Over and over again this rang throughout the city, followed by the sounds of hundreds of arrows gliding through the air. Finally, the sound of screams and roars finished the nightmarish melody.

*Thud thud. Thud thud. Thud thud.*

His heart pounded violently against his chest, reverberating throughout his body and crashing through his head. *I can do this... I can do this... I can do this,* he echoed.

Screeching metal rang out as the gate rushed open. People from all around him began sprinting towards the opening, leaving him behind in their wake. They rushed through the entrance, heading toward the walls as he stood motionless.

He watched as Rowan began darting towards the commotion. Jarren's heart sank in his chest at the sight, sinking deeper as his body disappeared behind the gray. He shook his head and winced at the sound of screams leaking out from the walls. His foot slowly inched forward before the other did the same. They repeated themselves over and over until he was running steadily to the walls. Warnings flashed through his mind with each step, urging him to abandon the cause and turn back before he ended up in a grave.

*Ding Ding, Ding Ding.*

Bells rang from the city, mixing harshly with the dissonance of the bells that followed shortly after. The sounds swarmed together to create a jarring ringing that echoed constantly in his ears as he ran.

*Di-ding, Di-ing, Ding, Di-ding.*

He crossed through the threshold of the city, gasping at the sight outside. Guards were attacking the people who had been the first to run through the gate as the rest spread into the area. The army was flooding upon the city walls as the commoners charged to keep them out. Bodies began dropping at the front of the commotion, although he wasn't certain which side's.

*Clang!*

He turned and looked up to find men in bright yellow slowly cutting through the mass of guards atop the walls, pushing them off the walls when they were swarmed and overwhelmed. His head snapped back to the ground at the sound of hooves trampling wildly towards them, thumping quickly against the stone floor below them. Horses trampled into view from the large path leading towards the castle, ridden by dark figures covered in hoods. Troops from all around watched fearfully as they positioned themselves to face more of the Black Cloaks, stepping in the center of the road as they raced nearer still. The people that had previously crowded the streets shrieked and ran from the road at the sight of the Black Cloaks approaching, and Jarren had the feeling that he should be doing the same.

Instead, he tightened his grip around his dagger and steadied himself, planting his feet on the ground as he refused to move. The walls might have fallen, but he was here now. And he wasn't going down without a fight. He would make Ezra proud, he decided. He wouldn't die a coward. He would protect her, even if it cost him everything. He would be the man he had always wanted to be. A hero.

The Black Cloaks plowed through the first line of troops, filling the streets with blood and screams. Two of the horses fell to the ground, crushing and trapping one of the riders, and flinging the other across the road. They were quickly killed by the people nearby as the rest swung relentlessly at the remaining horde.

He shrieked, stepping to the side as a body fell directly beside him, slamming into the ground with a thunderous clash as the armor connected with the stone floor. He whipped his head around and was knocked to the ground by a horse running beside him. A soldier turned at the impact and raised his sword high in the air as he neared him. His hands frantically searched the ground beside him, unsuccessfully trying to find the dagger that had flung from his hands when he fell. He flailed as he tried to crawl quickly backward, struggling to shrink away from him. Just as the man was almost upon him, a shiny arrow tip protruded from the blackness of his figure. His arm dropped and he fell from his horse as another appeared through his head. Jarren screamed as blood poured from the man, his body crashing down onto the ground as his horse ran haphazardly in circles.

Jarren dragged his eyes from the man's bloody skull and met the blue eyes of a young man, crossbow in hand. He rushed over to him and grabbed Jarren's hands, pulling him up from the ground and handing him the dagger he had picked up beside him.

"Come on," the young man said quickly as he strolled through the chaos.

Jarren scampered behind him, running from the mayhem surrounding him. He walked straight to a small gap between two buildings, slipping into the narrow alley.

"Damn these soldiers," he responded gruffly as he ran his hand through his short black hair, quickly darting his head back behind the wall. "It's been a long time since I've fought in a battle. Seems to be your first."

Suddenly, the man darted out from the wall and pierced his dagger into an oncoming soldier's chest. The man fell to the ground as he withdrew the weapon and wiped off the blood before stuffing it back in its sheath. He watched as red spilled out from the black pile on the floor, pooling around his body as Jarren stared in awe. It stained the remaining snow that clung to the ground, forever tainting it.

"Here," he said as he motioned for him to take back the dagger.

Jarren pulled his eyes up from the blood and wrapped his hand tightly around his dagger, his heart finally slowing in his chest. The man reloaded his crossbow as he stood, his body frozen as his mind raced. Jarren gulped as he watched through the gap in the walls, glimpses of black and flashes of bloodied bodies running back and forth.

"We can't stay here," the man said as he nodded his head for Jarren to follow.

He stepped out from the walls before turning back to look for him. Jarren's feet remained planted in the ground, refusing to leave the relative safety of the surrounding walls. All that he could hear was the pounding of his heart as he stared into the fighting in front of him.

"Go! You'll die if you stay," he shouted.

Jarren inhaled deeply, mustering the last bit of courage he could find. He closed his eyes tightly before quickly opening them and rushing out into the open, dashing towards him as fast as he could. The man shot a few more troops as they pushed through the frenzy, slowly lessening the yellow and black-covered bodies that filled the gray streets.

Jarren paused and stared down at the ground where a body lay, a haunting expression in his eyes. An old woman with gray hair and pale skin was covered in blood, a dagger resting in her chest. He stared at her as a soldier ran up to another man's back. He ran forward and plunged his dagger into the man's back repeatedly, crumbling him just before he had reached his target. Blue eyes turned as the body hit the ground, watching fearfully before looking up to meet his. Jarren's bloodied hand shook as he stumbled backward. His head spun, appalled at his actions and instincts of violence. He was a killer.

Another yellow figure approached and the blue eyes were ripped from his as he began to fight off more men. Jarren plunged his dagger into another man, watching as he fell to the ground. His head pounded and he turned to grab the man's sword.

He dropped the red-stained dagger and used both hands to grasp the weight of the heavy metal. Jarren had never wielded a sword before. The closest he had come was reading about them in his books.

Jarren turned and ran from the mayhem. He sprinted back towards the trees, needing to clear his head before returning to battle. He danced around the dead bodies and clashing swords littering the area, trying to avoid all confrontation as he moved. His heart sank at the sight of the countless peasants who lay motionless in piles of blood on the cold stone streets. He couldn't help thinking that he could've easily been in their place. He nearly had been.

He ducked into the cover of the forest, scanning his surroundings to check for any signs of movement. He was surrounded by trees and bushes that hung perfectly still, almost peaceful. The thick foliage and snow-covered branches quieted the horrendous noises that rang out from the other side of the wall. He swung the sword around repeatedly, frantically trying to grasp the motions. The troops would push past to where he was at any moment. He needed to be prepared when they did.

He slashed his sword left and right, clumsily attempting to cut down his imaginary targets. He then thrust it forward a few times before feeling steady enough to wield it. He had never used his dagger before and that had worked well enough. Jarren figured this couldn't be too dissimilar.

Jarren leaped behind the tree nearest to him when he heard heavy footsteps approaching. Sweat began dripping from his brow, causing his shaky eyes to burn. He peered around the bend and saw two men clad in yellow painted armor slipping past the gatehouse and heading east. If successful, they would soon arrive at Mourner's Row. Everyone that he had ever known or loved was there, hiding in fear. Everyone except Ezra. Ezra. His head swirled at the thought of her. Jarren wasn't sure whether it was the fear, the cold, or the adrenaline that caused him to shake, trembling amongst the stillness surrounding him.

Jarren darted out as they neared his position, thrusting his sword into the first man's chest. He quickly darted back, his tall frame and long limbs finally being of use to him. The other man raised his sword and charged at Jarren. He clumsily lifted his sword to parry the attack, barely bashing it out of the way in time. He stumbled backward on the frost-covered ground, tripping over the roots that weaved through the forest dirt. His back slammed into the ground with a heavy thud. The man stood over him and slashed his sword down at Jarren. He ducked back, narrowly avoiding the fatal blow. He quickly swept his leg up from underneath the man, knocking him onto the ground beside him. Jarren raised his sword and bashed it against the man's face, refusing to relent until his hand was sprayed with red.

Jarren finally rested, leaning back against the stark white forest floor. He lifted his hand, refusing to face the man who lay beside him. Slowly, he pushed himself up into a sitting position and surveyed the area once more. He was alone again. Whether or not Jarren survived, he knew that the person he once was had died.

# 17

# Jarren

He used a tree to steady himself as he slowly stood, his head swirling and his legs shaky. He coughed weakly, his body shaking with each hack. He examined the sword in his hands, tears beginning to slide down his cheeks. His body shook and his lungs shuddered, overworked and rough.

Bile rose in his throat and his mouth was filled with a salty taste. He turned quickly to his side and vomited at the sight. When his stomach was finally emptied, he wiped his mouth and raised his glance to survey the area. Soon enough more men would come his way. The main gatehouse had fallen and soon the streets would be flooded with troops.

He heard more footsteps rounding the corner and prepared himself for another fight. He wiped the tears from his eyes and shook the exhaustion from his body. He had no choice. He had to stand and fight. He needed to protect Ezra.

His breath hitched in his throat as he saw a dozen figures rounding the corner. He sighed a breath of relief when he saw that it was merely more commoners coming to defend the city. He was no longer alone. He wouldn't have been able to fight the army off by himself. He would have been easily overwhelmed, he thought. Now just maybe they would have a chance. Many of the troops must have died off approaching the castle. The Black Cloaks were trained archers. They had also fought off hordes of them as they approached the gatehouse. Beyond that, the commoners had killed hundreds of troops as they entered the city. There couldn't have been more than a few hundred left, he reasoned. Perhaps they could win.

One of the men lightly nodded at him as they went to stand beside him. They raised their weapons as they stared at the road leading up to the gatehouse. Silence fell over them as the sound of fighting grew nearer. He began to tremble once again, his head spinning and his eyes wide with fear.

"They're coming," the man said.

The sound of horses' hooves neared from around the corner. He sat against a wall, his head resting back against it. He breathed slow deep breaths as he stared at the cloudy gray sky above. A cold wind threatened to seep right into his skin, edging its way through his heavy tunic. He glanced down and looked at the Black Cloaks, sitting upon their horses. They dragged a small group of the remaining soldiers behind them, slowly making their way up to the castle.

He glanced down at his hands and surveyed the injuries he had sustained. A large scrape crossed down his left cheek that dripped blood down onto his heavy tunic. His hands were bloody and bruised and his knuckles were split open in places. His ankle had twisted during the fall and screamed of pain. He considered himself lucky, he was in much better shape than most.

He pressed his hands together, inspecting the wounds that littered them. He ran his hand over his cheek and winced at the pain. A small trail of blood had wiped off his skin and now covered his hand. He would escape the war with only a small scar. Perhaps he would look like a hero from his novel. All the great knights bore some sort of battle injury. Now he could consider himself a hero. He had faced his first battle and survived to tell the tale.

He sighed, his heart slowing in his chest. He wiped the blood off of his newly acquired sword and shifted his weight onto his unsteady feet.

He pushed up off the ground and winced, his back tender and swollen. He turned and began making his way toward Mourner's Row. He passed by the town square, stepping over bodies as he walked. A small snowflake fluttered down onto his cheek, followed by countless more. Soon a whole flurry dropped from the sky above. By the time he had returned home, a small white blanket covered the bloody streets.

"Mother, Father?" he called as he pushed open the wooden door.

He stopped abruptly as he entered the room, his father was kneeling and crouched down in front of him. Jarren made his way around him before nearly fainting at the sight. He had prepared himself for nearly everything he knew he would see that day. He tried to imagine what would happen if they had lost, if Ezra had been taken, if he had been severely injured. Yet, he never could have prepared himself for this.

He stared into the flames, watching as they grew into a steady roar. Tufts of gray smoke began climbing their way up toward the sky. Evelyn lay atop a large pyre outside Vaor's walls, piled high with wood from the surrounding forest. Jarren watched as the flames slowly engulfed her lifeless body, carrying her spirit into the supposed heavens above. He stared at her pale face and dark brown hair, now matted against her once beautiful features.

Only a few days ago she had been lecturing Jarren and slapping the side of his head to wake him in the morning. Now, she lay still, a picture of grace among the chaos of the flames surrounding her. He watched as the pyre began smoking heavily, the flames soaring and blazing a variety of yellows, oranges, and blues.

Rowan stood beside him silently, unmoving as he mourned his beloved. Jarren glanced up at the rising smoke, tears rolling down his flushed cheeks. He hoped that the legends and tales he heard growing up were true. He hoped that her spirit would ascend and that she would finally be able to rest. She deserved at least that, he thought.

Over the next few hours, they remained standing there, staring into the flames. Eventually, the fire subsided and only a pile of ashes and bone fragments remained. They began digging into the hard dirt, forming a small hole in the ground. They dropped the ash and bone down into the crevasse before filling the hole and patting the soil down. A tall tree stood next to her now-buried remains. Here, she would lay undisturbed and protected. Frozen tears spilled onto the ground, covering the area.

Jarren regretted everything that had happened that day. He wished that he had refused to fight against the army and instead had stayed to protect his mother. He despised himself for not standing up to them when they demanded he go and fight. Most of all, he despised the royals for starting the war in the first place. His mother shouldn't have died. The royals deserved to die. Not her. Soon enough they would, he echoed.

Jarren stood from the cold ground and turned to face his father. He offered him a small smile and began walking silently up the mountain toward the city. They passed by countless bodies as they started their ascent. His breath grew harsher as they climbed, his legs still tired and weak. His knees began to ache when they finally neared the city's stone walls. Arrows littered the ground around them and bodies had been piled into heaps to clear the pathway that led to the city.

They crossed through the main gate, now crumbling in many places. They weaved through the streets and back to their house. The door had been broken in and the window still remained shattered and in pieces. Jarren closed the door behind him and sat at the small wooden table in the corner of the room. He grabbed some leftover bread that he had taken home from the bakery and tore through the tough loaf, gnawing on the hard substance.

Jarren turned and looked at the small sack that lay on top of his bed. He had wrapped his new sword and hidden it away. Many of the Black Cloaks had died in the battle, however, they still controlled the city. He wouldn't risk them discovering his most prized possession. He needed someplace to hide it. Someplace it wouldn't be discovered if the Black Cloaks were to raid their house. Soon the freshness of the battle would pass and they would sweep the streets, scavenging whatever weaponry and armor they could find.

He swallowed the last chunk of bread and rose from the table. The last of the food they had stolen from the transport was nearly gone. It had kept them well fed, yet now was severely lacking. He would need to procure more if they were to continue on. His mother had always been the one to handle meals. Now, it seemed that he would be the one providing. His father had shut down completely and was of no use. He needed to be the strength that kept them alive, Jarren thought.

He walked over to his bed and lifted the package. He unwrapped the contents and admired the craftsmanship. It was a typical arming sword, one that most soldiers carried. The grip was made of wood wrapped in leather and featured a crossguard. Jarren smiled in awe of his possession. It was nothing special to any soldier, but to him it was incredible. For years he had dreamt of holding a steel sword such as this. Now, it was a reality. He held the sword and turned it over in his hands. It weighed only a few pounds, perfect for a man like him, he thought. His slender frame and long arms had made for a perfect combination for this sword.

Now, he could practice with it and become a great swordsman, he thought. He was one step further to becoming a hero. All great knights wielded impressive swords, which he now possessed. Now, all the sword needed was a name to match it. Something that exemplified who he was and what his mission was. He dreamt of using the sword to cut down the Black Cloaks and rid the city of the royals who poisoned it. Vengeance, he decided.

# 18

# Ezra

"Oliver!" she screeched as she ran across the stone floor, quickly closing the gap between the two of them. "You're alright!"

He wrapped her in a tight hug, lifting her off the ground. Ezra smiled as he placed her back down. She scanned him up and down, staring at his steel armor, now scuffed with scratches from the fighting.

"As soon as the battle was won I knew I must come see you. You were all that I thought of during the fight. I wanted desperately to get back to you."

Ezra fought off a smile and glanced quickly down at her feet as she spoke. "I was worried when I heard them charge through the gatehouse and up towards the castle. It was so loud, we thought they were practically right upon us. We were worried they had entered the castle."

"I would never have let them get that near to you," he said with a small smile. "The Black Cloaks are rounding up the last of the soldiers as we speak. The rest have all been killed. You're safe, my lady."

"Thank the gods we're alright. I'm so glad that you came to see me. I was so worried, my thoughts were consumed wholly by you," she replied as she played her part.

"I would have fought off the entire army myself to ensure your safety," he grinned.

She smiled as the women surrounding her swooned. Marcella passed behind him, smiling at Ezra as she passed by. She knew that all the women wished they were his betrothed instead of Ezra. Sometimes she even wished it herself, she admitted. Yet, she had been selected and it was now her duty to play the doting princess.

"I'm certain it was quite the battle, my Prince. I look forward to hearing you regale all about it after you've rested. I'm sure you must have wounds that need tending to."

"Thankfully my armor took most of them," he chuckled.

Ladies from all around the room echoed his laughter, gazing wistfully at him. Ezra smiled and turned from him, a small chuckle passing through her lips. He had battled no doubt, yet she was certain it couldn't compare to the thousands of commoners that fought armorless and weaponless beside him.

"Well then, I must admit I'm quite shaken up by today's events. Forgive me, your grace, but I must rest now."

"Of course, my lady," Oliver replied with a polite smile.

"Marcella, I must retire to my chambers," Ezra dismissed. "I look forward to seeing you at supper, my Prince."

She walked quickly from the room and began her journey up the winding stairs to her tower. With each step, she yearned to be walking out to the forest instead. She imagined running up to Jarren and wrapping him in a warm embrace. He was sure to have sustained injuries from the battle. He wasn't afforded the same weaponry and protection as Oliver had been. Her mind quickly descended into darkness. She trembled at the thought that he had suffered a much worse fate. She wondered if he had survived at all.

She jumped up the few remaining stairs and shoved open her door. She skipped over to her window and peeked down at the city below. Black and red dots littered the paths, crowding near the lower side of the city. The town square was in shambles, separating the upper classes of the city from the peasants that lined the outer edges of Vaor.

Jarren was somewhere inside these harsh walls outlining the city. She prayed that he had somehow survived the massacre that had occurred.

She couldn't fathom how many lives had been lost that day. Men and women had lived here for decades only to be cut down in a single day. Death had always seemed so distant. Yet now, it surrounded her.

She gaped out the frosty window, watching as the sun lowered and clouds covered the starry sky. The wind tugged at the branches of the trees far below her tower and gently swayed them back and forth.

She sat silently and played over her last interaction with Jarren. She had risked everything when she snuck out to see him. In return, he had yelled at her and insulted her betrothed. She had always known of his contempt for the royals, yet now it seemed she had learned its full extent. Jarren despised everyone here, she scoffed. Ezra, however, knew them to be much different. She saw them as people instead of figureheads. She had seen the queen's fear during the battle. She had seen Oliver's kindness. These were people, she thought; and he wanted them executed despite never having been in the same room with them. How was he any different, she questioned, if he became so apathetic toward violence.

"Ezra, may I come in?" Marcella knocked.

"What is it?"

Marcella peeked through the door before sliding into the room, shutting it behind her. She walked up and sat beside Ezra on the windowsill. They sat in silence for a moment as they gazed out over the city below. Smoke poured from the many buildings that filled the city and rose to the overcast above. Ezra sighed as she stared out over the city that she had once found to be quite beautiful.

"Oliver seems to have taken quite a liking to you," Marcella said with a small smile.

"So it seems," Ezra replied simply.

"If you don't mind my saying so, he seems to have brought a change within you. I notice you seem to enjoy your time within the castle more than you used to."

"What would make you believe that?" Ezra questioned.

"You sneak out far less often than you did before your engagement."

Ezra paused at her comment. She hadn't thought Marcella had noticed her absences. Ever since her family had returned to River's End she had been much more careful about leaving the castle. Ezra had wanted greatly to see Jarren far more regularly, yet restrained herself in fear of being discovered. If one of the Black Cloaks had caught her, she would have been taken in front of the King and Queen.

"That was my father's doing, not Oliver's."

Marcella shrugged, "Well, I envy you nonetheless. I imagine every lady of nobility has dreamt of marrying him."

"I never wanted to," Ezra admitted. "I never wanted to marry anyone, actually."

Marcella's eyebrow scrunched together in disbelief, "All of Vaor wants what you have. You shouldn't take it for granted, my Lady."

Ezra paused as Marcella nodded with a smile before strolling back over to the door. Ezra stared out the ice-cold window and watched the fluttering snow. Marcella was right, she thought. Every other woman in Vaor wanted to marry the Prince but her. However, her heart had already been won by another man. That man, she worried, might not have survived the battle. She ached at the thought of not knowing and desperately wanted to see him. Yet the feat was impossible with the swarms of people in the castle at the moment. She would need to wait until the chaos dissolved, she decided. Then, when the first opportunity arose, she would run to him. Until then, she waited with bated breaths.

Ezra paced her bedroom for hours before finally laying down to rest. She laid down upon the gaudy fabric and feather stuffed pillow. She stared up at the cold ceiling above her and listened to the wind howling as it wrapped itself around her tower. Slowly, she drifted off into another restless night's sleep.

*Her eyes ripped open at the sound of a harsh wind blowing through her. She sat on a jagged rock, wet and rippled with tiny pools of water. Dripping noises rang from far in the distant darkness. She strained her eyes to adjust or find some sort of light source. A faint chorus of voices mumbled incoherantly.*

*She slowly rose and stumbled through the pitch-black walkway as rocks scraped against the pads of her feet. Carefully, she tip-toed through the nothingness as the voices neared. She stalled as she heard the voices stop, hesitating at the sudden quietness. Faint whispers grew into chants once again as she closed her proximity to them. She saw a faint warm light emanating from around a bend in the rock passageway.*

*She crept around the edge and peered her head out from her hiding place. Raggedy shadows encircled a blazing fire, creeping around it in a twisted manner. The chanting stopped abruptly once again, to Ezra's dismay. The shadows turned towards her and hissed, lunging at her with misshapen bodies.*

*She screamed and turned to flee back into the darkness, only to find herself surrounded entirely. The cavern had returned to darkness, leaving her trapped in its cold embrace. She sobbed and closed her eyes, unable to stop herself from picturing the sewn-shut eye that haunted her.*

*A hand grasped at her shoulder, causing her to turn sharply. She turned to find Jarren, pale and bloody. His body fell to the ground, chasing the blood that dropped from him. She reached out and wrapped her arms around him, supporting his weight as he collapsed into her arms. She sat on the ground, holding him tenderly in her lap as she wept. She blinked and a tear fell from her eyes. She opened them and found herself once again trapped in a meadow, alone.*

Ezra leaped forward in her bed, her head swiveling to examine her surroundings. She stilled, her heartbeat thrumming in her ears. Her skin felt cold and clammy as she wiped the hair that had stuck from the side of her cheek. Tears rolled gently down her face as she bit at her knuckle and tried to steady her breathing. I'm safe, she repeated. I'm safe here. I'm alright.

She stirred in her bed, repeating the same mantra as her body slowly calmed. She turned and hung her feet off her bed and touched them down onto the frigid stone beneath her. She padded across the room and stopped in front of her fireplace. She froze as she caught sight of herself in the mirror. She looked pale and timid. It reminded her of the commoners that littered the streets, with their sunken cheeks and matted hair. She didn't look like herself, she thought.

She crossed over to the table and sipped water to cool her burning throat before resting back in her bed. She stared up at the ceiling as her mind clouded once again. She was afraid, yet she couldn't remember what of. The only thing that she ever seemed to remember about her dreams was the sense of dread and fear when she awoke. That, and the sewn-shut eye. She hoped that she would never see such a thing any-where other than in her dreams, yet, somewhere deep inside her, she knew that one day she would.

# 19

# Jarren

"Jarren!" Ezra shouted as she ran up to him, her cloak dragging behind her in the snow. "You're alive!"

He watched as a few tears slipped from her glassy eyes as she approached him. Ezra wrapped him in a tight embrace, pressing her head against his chest as she hugged him. A smile crept over his face at the warm contact.

"I've missed you," he replied.

"I was terrified that you hadn't survived. When I heard that they broke through the gates and nearly made it to the castle I was certain most of the men that were fighting had died," she worried.

"No. Not me at least. Rowan and I both survived…"

"I'm very glad. How is Evelyn doing? Was she as worried as I was?"

He lowered his eyes at the question. He had looked forward to reuniting with Ezra, yet the notion that he would have to inform her of his mother's passing had severely lessened the desire to speak with her.

"When the army breached the gatehouse many of them headed straight for the castle. The first area they crossed through was Mourner's Row. There were lots of casualties in Vaor. Many from the women and children that were left unprotected during the assault…"

"Jarren…" she replied, her eyebrows furrowed and her eyes wide.

"She didn't make it, Ezra. She's dead."

"I'm so, so sorry," Ezra said.

"We buried her a few days ago."

"Jarren, I know Evelyn and I were never very close. But, she'll be missed more than you know."

"I miss her so much already. She's only been gone for a few days but I can't help feeling like she's still here. I don't believe that she's gone sometimes," he replied.

"That's how I felt when my family left me here when I was young. I couldn't fathom the idea that I wouldn't close my eyes and awaken in River's End. Although that couldn't possibly compare to the grief that you must be feeling," she admitted.

He sighed heavily, "I can't stop replaying the last conversation I had with her. I told her that she was going to be alright. That we wouldn't let anything happen to her. That we would be safe and return to her. I made a promise to her that I couldn't keep."

"You were worried about her. You reassured her when she needed it. You were there for her when she needed you."

"No… I wasn't. I did whatever I needed to do. I risked my own life. I killed people. I did everything I could to protect the people that I love. And it still wasn't enough."

He leaned against a barren tree trunk, staring at the clouds rolling in the sky above him. He breathed in deeply, trying to calm down and stop crying. The sun was lowering behind the city's walls, casting bright streaks of colors into the sky. Moments like these he usually wished he could stay in forever, but right now all he wanted to do was escape. Escape this sunset, this moment, this entire day. This life.

"How did you sleep after you lost her? That first night without her," she asked with a shaky voice, looking into his eyes.

He smiled sympathetically at her, his eyes showing a trace of sadness. "I didn't," he sighed.

"I wish that I could have been here with you. I cannot imagine suffering through that all alone. These last few nights I've scarcely slept. I couldn't imagine looking out over Vaor and you not being a part of it."

"My father and I have barely spoken since. It seems that neither of us knows how to carry on. Am I supposed to pretend that everything's okay? Do I speak of her death and only remind us of the grief? We have always been distant and Evelyn held us together. Now that she's gone, it's as though we're an ocean apart."

"All I can say is this: allow yourself to grieve. These things won't resolve in a matter of days. Your father is the only person who knows how you feel right now. You might have more in common than you think. For now, just be. The rest will come," Ezra said with a small smile.

Jarren let out a small laugh as he turned to face her. He wiped a tear that spilled from his puffy red eyes. Ezra always had a way of making things seem so simple, he thought. If only life was truly as simple as she made it out to be.

"I don't think we'll ever reach a good place, Ezra," he admitted.

"Just speak with him. Tell him what it is you're feeling. Start with that. I spent years struggling to figure out my place here in Vaor. I refused to let go of my past and accept the fact that I couldn't go back. You've already lost one parent. Don't let this cause you to lose the other. At the end of the day, the two of you are all that you have left."

"I'll try. But, I'm afraid that he's too consumed with anger to even have a civil discussion. He's mad at the army for attacking. He's mad at himself for not being there to protect her. He's mad at the royals for starting this bloody war. All he knows right now is anger."

"Jarren, you have a way with words. You always have. He listened to you about the attack. He trusted you because you convinced him too. If anyone can get through to him it's you," she paused, her eyes brimming with tears. "You need to find a way to connect with your father. I can't leave you here to deal with her death all by yourself. It's too heavy a burden to bear. Let him share it with you. Drink to her memory and cherish the times that you had together. Don't throw away your life grieving hers. I wish more than anything that I could have been here for you. I deeply regret not being able to comfort you after the battle."

"I wish you had been here too," Jarren replied softly.

"I'm sorry. Oliver rushed back to greet me and make sure I was alright as soon as the battle was over. I couldn't sneak out... I wanted to."

He sniffled, rubbing his hands together as he stood from the tree he was resting upon. The cold has seeped its way down to his bones. He shivered and nodded for her to follow him. Slowly, they weaved through the forest and headed towards the town square.

All throughout the streets red stains covered the stones. It only stood as a reminder of what he had done. He was no better than a Black Cloak. He had always despised how easy it seemed for them to take someone's life. However, when the time came down to it, he was just the same, Jarren worried.

He led them through the streets until they came upon the chapel, still standing unharmed. Thankfully, many of the city's buildings had remained untouched. Mourner's Row was the nearest to the main gate, easily forgotten by those far up in their castle. It seemed fitting that it had been the first to fall, he thought.

"I thought you weren't religious?" Ezra questioned. "Jarren, why did you bring me here?"

He grabbed her hand and led her through the doors and up the pathway to the large altar that stood at the back of the chapel. He knelt down beside the altar and faced the rows of candle and incense that burned surrounding it.

"I came here before the battle. I lit the incense and prayed to the gods. I asked the Raven and the Dove for protection and safety. I begged them to spare us. To show us their mercy. I have asked nothing of them my entire life. And yet, when I needed them, they weren't there. Nothing can save us or protect us. Nothing in this world makes sense."

"Jarren-"

"Why should I connect with my father? Why should I do anything when it will all mean nothing in the end? We are all born here and die here and none of it matters anymore."

"Jarren, don't say such things. I know you must be angry, but please be rational. You mean everything to the people that love you."

"Who?" he said as he glared up at her. "My mother is dead, my father is gone with her, and I seem to have lost you as well."

"You know that isn't true! I will always be here for you. I left as soon as I could. I'm sorry, Jarren."

He turned, a tear welling in his eyes as he trudged out the door of the chapel and spilled out into the freezing winter air. He shivered and hastily made his way home through the thick snow that covered the ground, leaving Ezra frozen in the doorway.

He breathed in the crisp night air and paused as he neared his house. He stared up at the vast emptiness above him, a dark blue blanket freckled with bright white spots that stared back at him. His eyes traced shapes in the stars, pretending that they weren't simply thrown up there in no particular order.

He couldn't help but feel overcome with loneliness, struck by the fact that he was losing everyone he ever loved. Soon he would have no one left. He would be floating around aimlessly like the stars, swirling with no real direction or purpose. All he had now was his father. Ezra had been slipping away from Jarren ever since Oliver had gotten his claws into her. Evelyn's death had left a gaping hole in his chest that he worried would never be filled.

He sighed, closing his eyes as he listened to the crickets chirping in the distance. Their wings fluttered together, reverberating the music into the night sky. He chewed on his tongue, trying to keep himself calm as he breathed in the cold air surrounding him. Evelyn appeared in his mind, scared and fearing his life. He couldn't stop imagining what had happened to her, how she had felt. Thoughts trampled through his mind about all the possible ways that she could have been killed. Was she scared and tried to beg for her life? Did she call out for him or his father for protection? At least if he knew he would stop imagining her death over and over again, playing endlessly in her mind.

"Jarren, you're finally back," Rowan said gruffly, his blond hair coming into view as he pulled open the door and made his way into the room.

Jarren looked at him, sighing lightly as his father sat down beside him.

"Yes, I am."

"You were off with Ezra again?" he asked.

"Yeah, I was. We were talking about Oliver and everything that's happened recently," Jarren said.

"I thought you would be helping clean up after what's happened. Someone has to drag the bodies from the street."

"Last I checked that wasn't my responsibility. I think I've done more than enough for this wretched city."

"I just want you to start taking some responsibility around here. You're not a child anymore, you should be leading this revolt alongside me," he said as he waved his hands around, gesturing at Jarren.

"You know that's not what I want to do with my life, I don't want to follow in your footsteps," he replied.

"This discussion is not about what you want!" he raised his voice, walking back and forth in a line. "Life isn't all about you! Evelyn died because of the King and Queen. Countless people did. Don't you think its time to put an end to all the suffering?"

"There is more to life than violence and rebellion," Jarren spat.

"Our lives are about survival. That's what they have always been about, and that's what they'll always be about. It's selfish and naive of you to think that you can frolic around every day with no responsibilities and not a care in the world! We are some of only a small group of people that can save this city from collapsing in on itself. We owe it to the people of Vaor. We out it to your mother," he reasoned.

"Starting a rebellion against the King and Queen will only lead to more violence and more casualties. At what point does it end?"

"That's the reason!" Rowan shouted. "It will never end so long as they reign. The violence will never stop. They started this war! They are the reason she died! We need to take them out of power and take over control of Vaor. Otherwise, people will never stop worrying. People will never stop dying. This is the only way we can ensure that the people of Vaor will finally have a ruler who isn't willing to sacrifice them as though they don't matter. Although not ideal, sometimes you must end violence with more violence."

"It's time they died for once, not us," Jarren agreed, his lips pulled into a taut line. "At least that we can agree on."

# 20

# Ezra

She admired the intricate stone carving that outlined the mantle as the King drabbled on incessantly. Although she was rather used to his nightly dinner ramblings she had never been asked to speak with him outside of those meals.

"The solstice celebrations will begin in a fortnight according to the astronomers. This will mark the end of the dark night and signal the start of summer. I suggest it's high time we set a date for your wedding," King Henry said as he strolled through the throne room.

Ezra paused and glanced up at him as they walked beside the large mantle, feeling the warm flames against her. She pulled her lips into a small smile as she spoke, "Was there a date you had in mind, your Grace?"

"The solstice is this moon, I say you are to be wed the following full moon," he replied. "The gardens should begin harvesting then and we shall enjoy the first harvest meal then."

Ezra nodded briefly, her breath hitched in her throat at his words. She forced herself to stare straight ahead and make no ill remarks. This was her duty, she reminded herself. This is what she was born to do.

"I look forward to it, my King."

"Good," he said sharply. "It's done then. We will begin preparations after the solstice celebrations."

"My king," she said as she curtsied.

King Henry continued quickly down the corridor up into his chamber towers as Ezra watched, her smile fading with each step. Her face drooped and she stared into the flames, watching as though there would be something within them that could help her. She couldn't tell Jarren that the King had set a date. Jarren was already jealous of Oliver, she didn't need to give him any more reasons to quarrel with her.

She huffed and watched the inside of the stone fireplace twirling with color as it climbed up to the mantle. She had only so much time before the wedding would be announced and all of Vaor would hear the news. As much as she wanted to delay the inevitable, she needed to tell him before then, she decided.

Ezra turned and fled to the Eastern tower, climbing steadily up the stairs until she reached her chamber. She pushed open the doors and turned to the dresser beside it. There, she lifted the piece of parchment and quill that lay beside it and brought it to the table in the middle of the room.

To Kira Bale, Lady of River's End

Greetings my dearest mother. Although I have not seen you in quite some time, I picture you often in my mind. It seems so long ago that you and Father rode North to Vaor to visit me. Though your trip was brief, it greatly delighted me to see you all again. I regret to inform you that ever since your visit, the state of Vaor has continually worsened significantly. Recently troops from Brunshire marched on the city and Prince Oliver, the Black Cloaks, and many commoners were forced to battle them. I am thankful to announce their success in the war, and hence my reason for writing to you. Now that the war has come to an end and summer is fast approaching, the King has decided to announce my wedding date. The event will occur on the next full moon only a month after the solstice. Although I am rather hesitant towards this arrangement, I do intend on following through in my commitment. I do, however, have a few questions that I would appreciate being answered. Were you apprehensive toward your marriage to Father? Were you as nervous as I am now? Did you doubt him as much as I doubt Oliver's character? Although I know him to be true thus far, I do find myself wondering if he is truly as he presents himself to be. Please do not hesitate to respond, the wedding fast approaches. I look forward to your correspondence and upcoming visit to Vaor for my nuptials.

Farewell my dear Mother,

Ezra Bale


She sighed and placed the quill back on the table, rereading her letter before closing and sealing it with red wax. She had many more questions, but feared the letter may be intercepted and read before it made it's way to her mother. She knew that she was being watched closely by the Queen, although she didn't know to what extent. She remained seated there and stared blankly around her room. Soon, she would join the Prince in his chambers and this room would no longer be hers. Ezra had spent her years here longing to leave this room, now she cherished each moment she had left in it.

She ran her hands over her bedding and up across the stone walls, making her way over to the windowsill. This is what she would miss the most, she thought. From here she could see out over Vaor and imagine what life was like down below. She pictured herself running through the streets in raggedy clothes, free to do as she pleased. Ever since she had grown, she was followed nearly everywhere she went. If she was to leave the castle she required guards. If she tried to sneak out she would be punished by her father.

Ezra sighed at the distant memories spent down in the city. She smiled at the thought of Jarren and how often they used to climb the trees on the southern end of the city. Perhaps Jarren was there right now, somewhere deep in the trees that lined the wall. She was relieved to know that he had survived. She had always seen something more in him than just a commoner. He was destined for much more, she believed.

Perhaps Oliver had something more in him, too. Perhaps she was being far too critical of him. She believed that Jarren was truly destined for more and that he had more to him than people knew. If she could believe that of Jarren, why couldn't believe that of Oliver? She simply needed to cease being so harsh with him and allow him the opportunity to prove it to her. She had been much to quick to judge him, she decided. Olliver still had given her no reason to suspect him, although she detested his mother and father completely. Perhaps he was different. Jarren certainly was nothing like his father was. Rowan had always been calculating and violent, whereas Jarren was much more calm and levelheaded. Perhaps the same could be true of Oliver.

Ezra strolled over to her door at the thought of it and began descending the tower stairs. She crossed through the courtyard and headed over to the library. At this hour he should be studying with his tutor. There she would have a chaperone to approve of their discussions. Now that their wedding date would be announced, she needed to be much more proper about her visits with Oliver. All eyes would be upon them until their wedding. Gone were the days of private strolls through the gardens and visits to each other's chambers.

She arrived at the heavy wooden doors and pulled them open before pulling back the hood on her fur cloak. She scanned the space and admired the rows of shelves that filled the room. Tables were sat in the center with a few men sat around them, scribbling on parchment as they worked. A large chandelier hung from the ceiling, the candles illuminating the musty room. Books of all sizes littered the space, more than anyone could read in a lifetime, she figured. She paused when she noticed Oliver sitting in the corner, thumbing through a large leather bound book. Beside him sat an older man, nodding in approval as Oliver read to him.

"Good, good," the man said as he tugged at the scratchy long beard that hung from his chin. "You've memorized King Ballord's life and achievements, move on to King Powell."

"Ezra?" Oliver questioned as he glanced up from his novel.

"My Prince," she curtsied. "I didn't mean to disturb you. I only wish to inform you of news from the King."

He lowered his book and sat it on his lap, waving off the man beside him as he smiled at her. Ezra closed the few steps between them and sat at the bench beside him. She hesitated as she fiddled with the wooden table in front of her, scratching against its rough edges.

"It seems the King has set a date for our wedding."

"I'm delighted to hear that, my lady. When is it set for?"

Ezra looked up and met his gaze. Her cheeks reddened at the sight of his warm brown eyes accompanied by a dimpled smile. It was as if everything about him invited her in. Oliver was well-dressed and even more well-mannered. He was the perfect picture of charm and nobility, she thought. She was delighted at the thought of him truly being genuine. He seemed excited by the idea of marrying her. Perhaps she had been wrong about him after all. She returned his smile and was drawn in by his charming ways. She fought off every instinct to melt into his arms as he spoke.

"The next full moon, after the solstice," Ezra replied.

"Excellent," Oliver said with a wide smiled. "The flowers should just be starting to bloom then. The early harvest will be pulled in a matter of days for the solstice and shall be in full swing by our wedding. What a magnificent feast it will be."

A small smile pulled at her lips and she lowered her gaze to the table. "I'm so glad you're pleased with your father's doing. I must admit I was wary of informing you that he had set a date."

"Why would you think that, my lady? I'm delighted at the notion, of course."

"Well…" she stammered, "I've been a bit apprehensive towards our arrangement. We grew up together, you see. I never imagined that we would be wed. I suppose it's caused me to shift the way I feel about you. Even changed the way I think of you."

"Well I should hope so. You're older now, more mature. I should think it only proper that you be wed. I would think it would be most exciting to be betrothed to a prince, nonetheless."

"I suppose," Ezra hesitated, "When my parents left me here I was angry. All I wanted to do was leave. I spent most of my days dreaming of the time that I would one day cross back through the city gates and return to River's End. I never imagined myself remaining here for so long. When our engagement was announced it meant that I would spend the rest of my life here. I suppose that's what caused me so much apprehension."

"I see. It has nothing to do then with me? You don't fine me... repulsive?" Oliver laughed.

"No, no. Nothing like that, I promise. Ever since the wedding was announced I find myself much more content with my life here. I still wish to travel the world. Yet, I find this castle... and everyone in it, much more likable."

"I hope that's partly due to my efforts, my lady. I admit that I could sense your hesitation. It's rather rare that a royal couple would have the time to get to know each other that you and I have been afforded. I took it upon myself to romance you and demonstrate what your life in Vaor could be like. I wanted you to know that we're not so bad after all, us royals."

"You've been rather convincing in that matter," she chuckled. "I sincerely look forward to our wedding."

"As do I, my lady," Oliver said with a grin.

Ezra curtsied once more and left the room, nodding at the gentleman transcribing the many books that filled the room. Her heart was fluttering in her chest, her head still swirling at their conversation. He was excited by their wedding announcement, and she was too, she admitted. Perhaps a life in the castle would be something she could enjoy. She wouldn't have to want for anything, she thought. She would have a life of luxury and romance with the handsome prince. And someday, she would be Queen. She would be able to help influence Vaor and its laws and policies. She could help change the city for the better and restore it to its once magnificent ways. Jarren was wrong, she thought. His anger and resentment had greatly clouded his judgment. They didn't need to use violence and rebellion to fix the Vaor. All they needed was her. Now all she needed to do was convince him of that before it was too late.

# 21

# Jarren

Jarren walked through the streets of Mourner's Row and weaved his way toward the castle. The tournament grounds were littered with fanciful decorations and green and yellow ribbons. Bundles of flowers were hung from poles and a large table brimming with vegetables, delicate cakes, and wine stood before the noble's tent. He strained as he searched the surrounding area for any sight of Ezra, though he found none.

He sighed and plopped onto a nearby bench, staring mindlessly at the knight's donning their armor. It seemed the only way the people of Vaor knew how to celebrate was a combination of opulence and violence.

"Welcome," the King bellowed, "To our solstice celebrations! We have had a hard winter, no doubt, however, we have emerged through the other side stronger, to be sure. We have survived the winter and defeated our enemies, finally putting an end to the war. We have many things today to celebrate. One of which includes the wedding of my beloved son, Prince Oliver. A date has been set for him to wed Lady Ezra of house Bale. They shall be wed a fortnight from today on the next full moon! You shall all be invited to attend their celebrations that night, as I'm sure you are all thrilled at the news. The Queen and I look forward to the day, however, we have much to do until then. Let us celebrate the couple as well as our victory in battle and our survival of winter!"

The crowd roared in celebration, which Jarren presumed to be mostly about the start of the tournament and less about what the King had to say. He lowered his head and stared at the muddy ground below him. Ezra was to be married in only a month's time. Then, she would be lost forever. He needed to do something to prevent this marriage, it was his last chance to save her, he thought.

Finally, the knights mounted their horses and began their many charges toward one another. They raced back and forth, the sound of their battle echoing off the stone walls surrounding the courtyard. Jarren jumped when one of the lances pierced through a shield and knocked one of the knights onto his back. Cheers erupted from all around him, pulling him from his trance.

He scanned his surroundings, stopping him in his tracks when he caught a glimpse of bright red hair peeking out from the nearby tent. Ezra was here. He hadn't seen her since they argued. She looked starkly different now. Self-assured and confident. Hardly the scared girl he had last pictured.

He stared at her as she took her seat, grinning widely as she surveyed the crowd along with the platters of food in front of her. She seemed to be enjoying her noble life, for someone who complained of it often. She laughed and tucked a bright strand of hair behind her ear, turning her head to the side before standing. She took a small curtsy before Oliver's profile came into view.

Jarren's mouth dropped into a taut line, nearly rolling his eyes at the sight. Of course, it had been Oliver that had made her look so giddy. She had defended him and his honor the last time they had spoken. How could he not have seen how easily she had fallen for him? Jarren felt so foolish now that he had seen them together. They were the perfect match. Both beautiful and graceful, the picture of elegance and nobility. While he, on the other hand, displayed scars and a slender body. A peasant's body. Unlike Oliver, with his muscular physique and expensive clothing. He was no match, Jarren thought.

Ezra turned and caught Jarren's eyes, a small smile grazing her lips. His breath caught in his throat and he darted his eyes away. He had been caught staring at them, disgust all over his face. His cheeks reddened at the thought of it. Slowly, he turned back to face her. Oliver brushed a strand of hair away from her face, and Jarren's mouth dropped at the sight.

Ever since they were children Ezra had always been his closest friends. His greatest admirer, his escape from the world. Now, she was someone else's. It was clear to him now. She had been stolen from him. Whisked away by a handsome prince. Worst of all, the son of the King and Queen of Reina. Oliver had gotten everything he had ever wanted since birth. But that wasn't enough for him. He had to take the only thing Jarren had left in the world. His best friend. The love of his life, he admitted. He was done being the victim, he decided.

He stood from the bench and stormed off through the festivities. He pushed by people laughing and dancing to the music. He passed the colorful ribbons and lively decorations. He no longer cared about the solstice celebrations. This was a day he usually cherished. It was a bright moment after the past few dark winter months. But not this year. Now, it only reminded him of the loss he had suffered this winter. His mother, his friend, and now Ezra.


He stared out the bakery windows, wishing him to be anywhere else but here. It was impossible to focus on his work with Ezra and Oliver and the rebellion. He pushed the thoughts of her away. He remembered the way her hair shined in the sunlight. The sound of her laugh echoes in his head as thoughts of her began to swirl. He couldn't stop the thoughts no matter how hard he tried.

A sharp scream rang from out in the streets, neighing and shouting arising in the mix. He watched as people ran in the opposite direction, panicking in the chaos. He ran out to the street, shoving past people as they ran in the opposite direction, pushing him back as they went. He searched the area, trying to find the cause of the commotion. His eyes widened in realization as he started sprinting towards the origin. A small group of Black Cloaks were raiding a house just around the corner.

"Jeanne! Jeanne!" he shouted, trying to make his voice rise above the loud cacophony around him.

Her frail body was curled up on the ground beside the house across from hers. She sat there crying hysterically as a Black Cloak stood over her. He ran over to her, kneeling down beside her as he watched them throw various things around her house and out into the street. They threw her clothes into puddles in the street and under the running feet all around them.

"Shhh… It's going to be okay," he said gently, glaring at the man beside her. "Why are you doing this? She's done nothing to deserve it!"

The man raised his head, his cold, dark eyes meeting Jarren's.

"Maybe not, but her son was found sneaking apples from the royal courtyard."

"How does that justify searching her home? You caught him in the act," he reasoned, "There's no need for any of this."

"We have to make sure she's not hiding any other stolen property," he said, a smug grin on his face.

"Where's my boy? What have you done with him?" she questioned deliriously.

"The King and Queen's new laws list that the punishment for thievery from the noble family is death," he said coldly.

"No!" she screamed, shouting numerous other unintelligible words at the Black Cloak.

She erupted into a hysterical sob, weeping loudly and burying her face in her hands. He hugged her, not knowing what to say. Tears rolled down her puffy cheeks, dripping quickly to the floor below. Onlookers gasped, whispering and pointing as they rushed past her. The Hunters walked out of her house and over to where they were sitting.

"We're all finished in there. She has nothing to hide."

The man mounted his horse and rode back toward the castle, turning back to look at them as he left.

"My boy! My poor boy!" she shrieked, sobbing as he held her.

"I'm sorry. I wish there were something more I could do. You certainly don't deserve this."

He sat there and comforted her as people returned from their houses, checking on her and looking in curiously at her house. Papers and clothing were scattered around, lying in the street and on the floor. Broken furniture pieces were strewn about and her bread lay soaked in a muddy puddle, squished and sopping with brown water.

"I'm sorry. I'm so, so sorry," he mumbled helplessly, "I'll go tell Shea of what's happened, he can take over the bakery and I will come right back and straighten up your house."

He spent the rest of his afternoon walking through the streets and picking up articles of clothing, rearranging and fixing her broken furniture, and trying to restore her house to its previous order. He walked with Jeanne as she went to her other son's place of work and told him the horrible news. He reassured her that everything would be okay, and hugged her every time she began to cry. He walked her back to her house as she sobbed hysterically. The entire time, he couldn't stop thinking that his mother had been right. Jeanne wouldn't be the only person to have her life ruined by the Black Cloaks. There would be many, many others. He needed to find his father, he needed to plan. It was time, he decided. He was ready.

# 22

# Ezra

Sunlight reflected off the snowy river that covered the forest floor. She trudged through the layer and ventured further into the forest. With each step, she felt heavier, the weight of everything on her mind slowing her as she neared him. A cloaked figure emerged from behind a row of thick greenery only a few feet ahead of her. A scowl formed on her face as she braced herself for the conversation to come. She huffed as Jarren's face came into view, turning to face her as her heavy steps crunched through the snow.

She froze as she entered the small clearing, staring into Jarren's sullen eyes. His usually bright brown eyes shimmered as if tearful. Before, his presence had always caused a warm stir within her, although it had now vanished completely. His once fluffy brown hair which she had loved to tussle now hung limply on his forehead. His narrow frame now seemed to overshadow her with his heavy presence. His easygoing ways had changed into a cold exterior, void of the childish ways she had grown accustomed to. A breath caught in her throat at the sight of him. She felt her resolve slipping, willing herself to push forward and confront him.

"Ezra," he breathed.

"I saw you earlier. Then, I turned away for a moment and you had vanished. I wanted to speak with you. Why did you leave?" she questioned.

"You know why I left," his eyes turned sour as he spoke, "I left because of him."

"You're jealous of Oliver?"

"Of course, I'm jealous of him! He stole you away from me! We were friends, Ezra. For years it was just the two of us. Then all of a sudden you get engaged and you're swooped away into his arms. It's as though all you ever wanted was a handsome lord to come and rescue you! Well, you certainly got what you desired. Now the two of you can live out your lives in the castle together and you can forget about all the time you spent scrapping with the peasant boy," he scoffed.

"Jarren, stop! I know that you're hurt, seeing us together in that way. You know that I never thought of you as just a peasant boy. You were my escape from the castle and my only friend at times. We dreamt of living completely different lives than what we were born into. At some point, you need to realize that those were just dreams, Jarren! We can pretend all we like but at the end of the day, it simply isn't real. We will forever be stuck in these lives and I will forever be stuck inside the castle. My engagement to Oliver means that I will never be able to run away like we dreamed of doing. I am doing the best I can with the circumstances I was born into. I suggest you do the same."

"You took the first man who showed you any attention and threw yourself into his arms. Oliver only wants to be with you out of obligation. If his mother wasn't forcing him to be with you, he never would be."

She gasped at the remark, fire stirring inside of her. His face was wild with anger, his eyebrows tucked in deep over his eyes. She shuddered, wishing that she had never visited him at all. Perhaps he simply was too far gone, consumed by the grief and anger he felt at his mother's passing, she thought. He had never shown her a display of rage like this before. Now, she worried that she was seeing his true colors. She inhaled a shaky breath, preparing herself before responding. She resolved not to let her anger consume her as it had with him.

"It is my duty to be with Oliver and to keep up appearances. His duty is to do the same. You're right. He and I wouldn't be together if it wasn't arranged to be that way. However, that is the reality I live in. I did not choose to be with him, however, now that I am, I will do my duty and play the part."

"So you're content then to be the princess of Vaor. You're telling me that you're actually happy with him? How many times have I heard you complain about the royal family? You've said a thousand times how much you wish to be rid of them. Now you're becoming one of them?" Jarren spat.

"Soon the King will have passed on, and Oliver will become king. He is a good man and he will make an excellent king. The two of us will rid the city of its outdated policies and wretched laws. Together, we will restore Vaor to its proper glory."

"What a lovely speech that is. Is that what you're planning on telling the people, then? You'd watch as they starve to death and are hanged by the Black Cloaks rather than do anything about it? You may have the luxury of waiting for his death, but the people of Vaor are suffering. We don't have the same privilege that you do."

"Do you genuinely believe I don't know that? You have constantly reminded me what a horrid person I am simply for not struggling as you have. How can you judge me when just like you, I did not choose this life? You want everyone to have better accommodations, plenty of food, and clothing, yet you hate the people that have it."

"How is it fair that you feast on roasted boar and slosh down wine while we starve to death? I only want to end the suffering, Ezra. If that means a few wealthy men lose their overstuffed heads, so be it."

"Haven't enough people died, Jarren? When will it be enough? How many people's lives need to be ruined for you to finally feel adequate?" she said, her voice quivering.

His eyes turned hateful as he stared at her. Ezra held her breath as she waited for his response. She hadn't meant to insult him like that, she thought. She had always known that he felt inferior to her. She never understood why before, the titles had always seemed so meaningless. Now, she felt the true extent of it all.

"How could you say that to me?" his voice broke. "My father always reminded me of our status. But, I never thought that you, of all people, would use it against me."

"Jarren, I-"

"It's time for a change, Ezra. We peasants are tired of waiting for empty promises to be fulfilled. It's time we take our fate into our own hands."

"Jarren, please. If you try to overthrow the King and Queen, you will lose, and many good people will die. Many of the people in the castle are good people. Myself, Marcella, Oliver-"

"The King and Queen deserve to die for all the people they've killed. How many people have died for them? Thousands? They started a war and forced the people to fight it for them. Then, when they were vulnerable, they forced the few of us left to fight for them. They don't care whether we live or die. The only thing they care about is themselves and protecting their riches. They have no business ruling a kingdom. Why shouldn't we find a better man to lead us?"

"If you begin executing people, you will be no better than they are. How many people are you willing to kill to achieve this goal? However many it takes? Even if you were successful, who is to say that an even worse ruler wouldn't emerge? What righteous man have you all chosen to rule Vaor?"

"My father is set to lead."

"Rowan?" she scoffed. "He's emotional and holds grudges easily. He couldn't hold the throne for very long. After a rebellion, the crown usually changes hands numerous times. We witnessed it in Brunshire before the war. Once the people started killing, they never stopped. What will you do if that happens here? This could become a pathway to neverending violence, and your father will be the next target."

"What do you suggest we do? Nothing? I will not let these people die, Ezra!"

"Why does it have to be you, Jarren?" she said, her eyes softening. "If not me, then who? If not now, then when? You may be content waiting for the future, too scared to do anything about it, but not me. I've faced battle and emerged victorious. My mother died for the King and Queen, and Merric did the same. I refuse to let those I love perish beside me. Even if there's hardly anyone left anymore."

She stalled at his words. His anger was coming from a place of pain. She was certain of it. He had turned his grief into anger towards the royals. He was completely unreasonable and unwilling to listen to a voice of logic. He was dangerous, she worried. He was dedicated to a violent cause. Without his mother, Rowan was the only driving force behind his decisions. His father hated the royals more than anyone, she thought. The two of them were unchecked and had nothing left to lose. They would die for this cause. She was sure of it.

"I don't want to lose you, Jarren. I don't want any part of this. You only have one life, Jarren. Don't throw it away by playing the martyr. If Evelyn was here, she would tell you to be patient. She would caution you not to be rash."

"But, she isn't here anymore. Don't you understand that this is the point of it all? Everyone in Vaor has mourned their loved ones because of the royals. It's time they died for once. Now, we'll make sure they do."

Tears welled in her eyes before spilling out over her cheeks. He pushed past her, his dark cloak sweeping past her as it trailed behind him. She turned and watched through hazy eyes as he stormed into the forest, his figure disappearing behind the frosted wooden walls. She worried that she had lost him forever. She had foolishly hoped that she could persuade him to listen to her. The friend she had confided in countless times now had no love for her. Jarren was right, she thought. She was now loved only out of obligation. She truly was all alone in Vaor.

# 23

# Jarren

He trudged through the snow, his body willing him to go back and his mind pushing him further away. His insides ached at the words he had spoken. His breath grew ragged as he started to gasp for air. His head pounded, causing him to pause and catch his breath. He leaned against a nearby tree, resting his head against the bark as he stared upward. The light blue sky draped overhead, a cold wind blowing across his tear-stained cheeks. He sunk his head down into his hands and tried to slow his breathing. His thoughts raced on as he tried to focus on his breathing. He worried that he might hyperventilate at the rapid pace he sustained.

His head snapped up, his breath halting at the sound of a nearby twig snapping sharply. Ezra's white fur cloak brushed through the woods in the nearby distance. Her footsteps were accompanied by the sound of sniffling. His heart tugged at the sound of her crying. He was the cause of her suffering, he reminded himself. He knew that he had hurt her with his words, but it seemed he only now had realized the extent of the damage he had done. He hated the circumstances that surrounded them. He hated Oliver for poisoning the mind of his only friend. He hated himself even more for ruining the best relationship he had. Ezra had been the only one that was always there for him throughout the years. Evelyn had tried, and now she, too, was gone. He had no one left. This was all his fault, he thought.

Jarren started towards her, willing himself to swallow his anger and reconcile with her. He walked quickly through the trees, following her through the jagged pathway interweaved with overgrown shrubbery. Her fiery hair came back into view as he rounded a large tree. He moved to close the gap between them when he overheard her mumbling under her breath.

"He's hopeless! Oliver would never treat me like this," she muttered.

He stopped abruptly at the mention of Oliver. He had been right after all. She really had fallen for the Prince. His heart turned icy at her cold remarks. She thought that he was hopeless, unredeemable. He had never needed saving, he thought. It turned out that she was the one who needed saving. Once they overthrew the King and Queen, along with Oliver, she would finally see that he was right all along. They were poison, all of them. If he could get Oliver's claws out of her, perhaps she would come back to him. Ezra would be his again, and Jarren would be free of the wretched Prince. Then, they could live the life they had always dreamed of. They could spend their days traveling the world, financed by Rowan after he became the ruler of Vaor. He could see it clearly now; it all seemed so simple. If they could take the castle and kill the King and Queen, Ezra would be his once again.

He slowed, continuing to follow her as she twisted and turned through the woods before emerging out onto the city streets. Ezra had escaped the castle, he thought. After Merric was caught, they sealed off the only entrance that Jarren knew of. However, if Ezra had snuck out of the castle, she must have used another route, he reasoned. If they were to take the castle they would need to find an alternate way in. Perhaps by following her, he could find another way in. Then, he could lead the charge into the castle. He would be the hero who stormed the palace and saved his princess. This was his chance. All he needed to do was follow her back to the castle and discover her secondary way in.

He darted his way through the streets, following her as she led him up through the city. They made their way toward the Eastern side of the castle, nearing the castle walls without attracting attention. He paused as she came into a large clearing, crossing to the other side before tucking back into a hallway pressed up against the outer wall. He followed across the street, hesitating before shuffling into the corridor. He squeezed between the walls and shuffled down the path before forcibly turning the corner. Before him stood a small door up against the very side of the castle. This must be used for transporting goods in and out of the castle, he thought. He stuck his hand out, only to find that the door was locked. Ezra must have stolen a key. They would either need to do the same or pick the lock. Finding someone who could pick locks could be a problem, he wasn't sure if anyone in the rebellion had the skills.

He quickly turned and darted back through the trees. If they wanted to use this entrance into the castle, he couldn't be discovered lurking nearby. He couldn't risk drawing any unnecessary attention to the door. He trampled his way through town before making his way back home. If he was being watched, he needed not to look suspicious. He was simply wandering through the town, nothing more. Finally, he made his way back home and slipped through the doorway before crashing down onto his bed. He needed to speak with his father, but first, he desperately needed to sleep. He hadn't been well rested since before his mother had passed. Now, he feared he wouldn't be able to sleep well again until Vaor had fallen. Until Ezra was his again.

# 24

## Jarren

"I know that recently we've lost a lot of people we've loved. Times have been hard on all of us and unity throughout this change is of utmost importance. We've grieved as a people and endured more than we thought we ever would. As the times change, I think it may be time for a change ourselves. I propose that we move into a new age where we won't have to live in fear. That we attack the castle in a fortnight."

Gasps and whispers erupted from all around the room, people shouting to him, cutting him off. Hands shot up as he raised his hands to silence them, trying to regain peace.

"Instead of sitting here waiting for the day they attack us, we need to be planning and preparing. They rule with cruelty and fear, killing anyone who opposes them. No one inside the castle has the power to do anything about it under their watchful eyes within the walls, but we do. I say we avenge those they have taken from us and prevent them from picking anyone else off. I say we do what we should have done long ago and end their tyrannical reign! I say we rise up, take control of our future, and make them pay for what they've done to us!"

Jarren stared at the ground, tuning out the noise bellowing from all around him. He proposed this plan as though it would end death, not lead them right to it. This could only mean more suffering, but what other choice did they have? His father was right, he thought. If they didn't do something now, they would all die anyway.

"A royal wedding is set to take place on the full moon at the chapel. The prince, Oliver, is set to wed a lady, and therefore, the entirety of the royal family will be attending. They each will take their usual heavy details of Black Cloaks along with them. This, along with the dozens more that will be guarding the chapel, will lead to our opportune moment. While they say their vows, we shall use this opportunity to sneak into the castle and begin the assault. We will face much fewer numbers this way and should be able to take the castle from within. Afterward, we will move one by one until we reach the chapel where we will take the royal family."

Silence fell upon the tavern as Jarren's heartbeat started increasing rapidly. Now was the time when he should speak up. Now was his last chance to stop him. To say something. Yet, he couldn't. He refused to let his love for Ezra interfere with this. These people had been waiting for a chance to free themselves. He couldn't ruin the first chance they had in such a long time. He couldn't... he reminded himself.

"We have discovered another entrance to the castle. After Merric was discovered and captured, the Black Cloaks sealed off the entrance they had used. We believed this to be the castle's only point of weakness. That is, until recently. My son, Jarren, discovered another entranceway that we will use to invade the castle. This, in combination with the wedding, is how we secure our victory. Our freedom. This is our chance," Rowan roared.

Cheers rang out from around the tavern, and people clanged their mugs together, ale pouring heavily. Men from all around the tavern swarmed around him, patting him on the back and welcoming him as one of their own. A smile overcame his face as he stared out over the group. For years, he had watched from the sidelines, listened as they schemed. Now, he was the planner. He was the soldier. He was the hero.

He sat at the chest, practicing the motions he had perfected over the past month. His father had managed to procure him a lockpicking set, although he wasn't sure how. He had been too afraid to ask his father when it had been given to him. All he needed to do was unlock the door on the eastern wall and the plan would be set in motion. He shuddered at the thought of all the responsibility. If he couldn't get that door open, everything would fall through. They would probably be discovered and captured. They would be put to death for their treason. He had to get the door open; he had to be perfect. However, the only thing he could practice on was a small chest with a lock similar to the one on the door, as far as he could remember.

If he and Ezra had still been friends, perhaps she would have simply given him the key. However, now, even if he asked, she would probably refuse. It had been so long since they had spoken that he wasn't entirely sure whose side she was on anymore. More time with the royals had corrupted her mind even further; he was sure of it.

He was the only hope she had to restore her to her former self. To rip her from their cruel grasp. Whatever it took, he was going to kill them. He was going to get her back.

# 25

# Jarren

His fingers moved deftly, quickly breaking through the lock that stopped them from their victory. A small clicking noise came from within the lock and a smile broke out on Jarren's face.

"I did it. We're in," he said with a smile.

He stepped to the side and let Rowan take the lead. Although he now had some combat experience, the Black Cloaks were much stronger and more well-trained than the soldiers he had previously fought. He lifted his sword and prepared to charge through the door. Most of the Black Cloaks had gone to protect the royal family. They estimated that only twenty or so of them remained inside the castle. Each of them only needed to defeat one or two in order for them to take the castle.

Quietly, they entered single file through the narrow passageway that led to one of the halls. Jarren tried to make sense of his surroundings, remembering back to the times when Ezra had described the layout of the castle to him. If only he knew how important those stories and descriptions would be to him now.

"We should come upon the great hall next. If we take the stairs, we should reach the main castle walls. Most of the guards should be positioned along them."

"I'll take most of the men up; you lead a small group to the throne room and then throughout the castle. Kill any Black Cloaks that you see and try to do so quietly. If they ring the bells, it will alert the Black Cloaks at the church. We cannot let that happen. Do you understand?"

Jarren nodded. "I'll meet you at the main gatehouse when we're through. Make sure you seal it off as soon as you're done."

"Good luck," his father replied.

He signaled the rest of the group to move with him, leaving only a few men behind. There were the Darby boys, Edward and Jonah, and a few others that Jarren couldn't remember the names of. They had all been introduced to him before, but his mind had been so focused on the battle that he couldn't seem to remember them. Jarren feigned a small smile as he scanned the group in front of them. This was going to be a real test of his bravery. He was leading a group now. He was in charge of their lives, and they were counting on him. Now was his turn to be the hero.

"Let's move. We should be nearing the Great Hall, afterwards, we'll make our way through the kitchen and into the throne room. Most of the guards inside the castle should be there."

The few men surrounding him all nodded in agreement before turning to follow behind him. He swiftly made his way through the hallway, scanning his surroundings as he entered into the Great Hall. Large tables lined the hall, with the biggest table seated higher than the rest. That one must be for the royal family, he reasoned. He pictured Ezra sitting up at the table, sitting next to Oliver and the King and Queen. He immediately tried to shake the thought from his mind. Ezra was getting married, perhaps this very minute. He had no time to hesitate. This was their only chance.

He crossed through the threshold and made his way past the table, scanning the doors that led to the courtyard to ensure they hadn't been discovered. He crept up to the doorway that led to the kitchens and peeked around the corner. The men followed swiftly behind him, double-checking all of their surroundings as they went.

He froze when a woman crossed by, entering what he could only assume was the pantry. He paused briefly as she turned a corner and went down a narrow stairway. He darted through the opening and crossed quickly into the kitchens. Food was spread along the tables, half-chopped in preparation for tonight's reception. They needed to hurry before she came back to finish the job, he reminded himself.

He peeked through the solid wood door that blocked them from entering the throne room. He could see two guards posted at the door that led to the courtyard. More could be inside, just out of his view, he reasoned.

He held up two fingers, signaling to his men. They would need to cross the hall quickly if they were to keep themselves hidden. He took a deep breath, preparing himself for what was to come. He was going to have to kill again.

He barged through the door and sprinted toward the guards. When he was halfway through the room, the guards turned at the noise. They raised their swords barely in time to parry his thrusts. He clashed his own down upon them and knocked one to the ground. He drove his sword down on top of the man and let out a deep exhale. The man to his left was knocked backward by Edward, who plunged his dagger into the man. They all stood silently for a moment as they stared at the scene before them.

"Let's get moving. Someone might come along soon and discover them."

"Right," Jonah nodded.

They turned and made their way over to the western tower. There, they heard voices descending the staircase.

"Did you hear that?" one of the voices asked.

Jarren slashed his sword just as he saw a dark-cloaked figure enter the room. The man fell to the ground with a grunt as Jarren leaped back. The other man paused when he saw the commotion and turned to run back up the staircase.

Edward quickly followed him up the stairs, his brother in tow. A quiet shriek echoed from the tower before a few moments of silence. Jarren stirred at the sound. He prayed that no one else would hear the commotion. Jonah slowly descended the staircase, a solemn look on his face.

"They're dead. Both of them. I wasn't there in time to save him."

Jarren placed a hand on his shoulder. He gave him a small smile as if it would help ache his grief. Jarren knew what it was like to lose someone. He couldn't save his mother when she needed him. He ripped his mind away from his mother. Now was not the time, he thought. Now, he needed to save Ezra.

"Let's keep moving," he repeated.

Slowly, they made their way through each hall, finding only a few Black Cloaks scattered throughout the castle. Their plan had really worked, he thought. They were going to take the castle.

*Ding-Ding, Ding-Ding.*

The sharp shriek of bells pierced his ears. He hadn't met his father in the courtyard yet. Were the bells a warning for them or for the Black Cloaks, he wondered.

"We're not sure that they've taken the castle yet. I say we work our way back through the castle and take the western tower up to the walls. They should have cleared that area already. It's the safest way to get to the bell tower."

They raced back through the castle, brushing past the litter of bodies behind them. He couldn't think about all the deaths he had caused. Not now. He frantically shoved open the door to the walls. Black Cloaks were lying face down on the walls. His father had already been through here. Why did the bells ring, he questioned.

"The bell tower is this way," Jarren called.

He ducked down when he saw the bell tower come into view, crouching behind the stone walls for as much protection as they could give him. He saw his father slowly approaching a guard in the tower, circling around the large brass bell. He slipped around the sight and caught the guard in the back with his dagger. They had been successful. They had taken the castle.

A small smile crept over his face as he stood from his position, slowly walking towards his father. He broke into a jog and wrapped him in a hug.

"We did it," Rowan said. "Now, let's hope that we can take the King and Queen.

"I heard the bells ringing. Did they see you coming?" he questioned.

"No," his father said with a sigh. "Ezra is married now. That's why they rang the bells."

Jarren's smile quickly faded from his face. How could he have forgotten about the wedding? He had been so focused on the mission that he had forgotten about the distraction. A small part of him had hoped that they would storm the church before the ceremony had been completed, he realized. Now, Ezra was gone, too. He needed to see her, he decided. He needed to give her one last chance.

# 26

# Ezra

She stood in the mirror, admiring the way her satin dress hung off her shoulders and clung to her sides. The light blue fabric accentuated her bright red hair, making a breathtaking stark contrast. Her mother stood beside her, a wide grin on her face.

"This is all I have ever wanted for you, my dear. I hope you know that we only ever wanted the best for you here. I am so glad that you have found happiness with Prince Oliver here in Vaor. You will make a great ruler one day." Kira grinned.

Her smile slowly faded as thoughts of Jarren swirled into her mind. She thought of her new married life and how he would be a changed woman. The life they had once shared seemed so distant now. Perhaps that's how he felt, stuck in time and left behind. She shook the thought deep into her mind, away from today's festivities. Today was supposed to be the happiest day of her life, she reminded herself. Today was going to be perfect. She would play the perfect princess, the perfect wife, the perfect lady, she thought.

"Are you still nervous about your nuptials?" Kira asked.

"I am," she replied, nodding her head slightly, "I'm unsure of what to expect. And to stand up there with all those eyes on me. I never thought the day would come when I would get so much attention."

"I understand," her mother replied calmly. "I felt the same way you do now when I was to wed your father. Just know that you are stronger and braver than you think. Whatever your marriage will throw at you, you are strong enough to make it through. I promise that you are ready for this day, even if you aren't so certain."

"My Lady, your carriage has arrived, we must make our way to the church," Marcella said as she entered the room.

Ezra nodded her head shakily as she slowly descended the steps and weaved her way through the castle. Cheers erupted as she made her way over to her carriage, drawn by two white horses. She gracefully slipped onto one of the red seats, surrounded by the gold embellishments that covered the carriage both inside and out.

Her hands shook in her lap as she focused on her breathing. Marcella and Kira climbed in and sat opposite her, smiling politely. She scraped at the pads of her fingertips as the carriage slowly began to move forward. She was headed to her future, she promised herself.

"Lady Ezra of House Bale, the Raven, and Dove call upon you today. Will you act as their servants in this marriage and put them first as you enter this covenant? Will you always remember who brought you life and who will take it away from you? Will you allow the Dove's mercy to wash you of your uncleanliness and become reborn a married woman?" the man asked.

"I will," Ezra replied, her voice quiet but steady.

She looked around at the hundreds of faces that surrounded her. Smiles beamed on all of the royals' faces. All except Queen Arabella, who appeared almost sad, she thought. She snapped back to look across from her. Prince Olver was gazing lovingly into her eyes. This was all most women dreamed about. But it had never been her dream. Yet, it was her reality nonetheless, she reminded herself. This was her duty. This was her place.

"I vow to let Prince Oliver lead us through our marriage and through all our hardships. I pray to the Dove for a peaceful and merciful marriage. May we be blessed with many children and many years together. I pray to the Raven for a long life of happiness. May we always remember our humble beginnings in front of the gods," she said with a small smile.

This was her duty.

"Prince Oliver, the Raven, and Dove call upon you today. Will you act as their servants in this marriage and put them first as you enter this covenant? Will you always remember who brought you life and who will take it away from you? Will you allow the Dove's mercy to wash you of your uncleanliness and become reborn a married man?"

"I will," he said, his eyes glimmering with joy.

"I vow to lead Princess Ezra through our marriage…"

Her thoughts drifted back to Jarren. She had never imagined marrying, although, she admitted to herself, she occasionally fantasized about running away with Jarren. Marrying him and starting a simple life together across the ocean. But those were only fantasies. This was her duty.

"I pronounce you both wed. Please step into the water," the man said.

Oliver grabbed Ezra's hand and placed it into the crook of his arm. She let out a small exhale as he led her toward the pool of water. Slowly, they submerged themselves in the flowing water, dipping backward until their heads touched the ice-cold water. She remained there for a moment, staring at the intricate ceiling above her. Slowly, Oliver pulled her up from the comfort of the water. Thunderous cheers erupted from all around them as they stood, staring into each other's eyes.

*Ding-Ding, Ding-Ding.*

The church bell rang, nearly covered by the cacophony of praise surrounding them. She smiled and turned to face the crowd, waving briefly before once again taking Oliver's arm. She noted the Queen's absence. Ezra stared in disbelief at the thought of his mother not having the decency to stay through the ceremony. Had the Queen hated her so sincerely that she had rather left than see her only son married to her, she thought.

*Clang!*

The door burst open, and three dozen men poured in through the walkway. They raised their swords and quickly surrounded the church. A dozen Black Cloaks drew their swords, only to be rapidly cut down.

Screams erupted from around the room as people tried to flee. Ezra stood frozen, mouth agape at her surroundings. She clenched tighter around Oliver, still sopping wet. She felt heavy, unmovable. She stared as one by one the guards were overtaken. The screams slowly died down as many of the guests ran from the church. Now, only the rioters and the royal family remained.

A silence filled the room that had once been filled with screams. She stood, shaking, wondering if it was from fear or the cold water. Had they come to kill them all? Surely, the Queen had called for more guards when she heard the commotion. Or perhaps she had merely left them behind to die, Ezra thought. She shook the thought from her mind. Surely, the Queen wouldn't be so cruel. She would never have left her beloved family behind. Then again, she had left during her own son's wedding. Maybe she had left them all to die, she worried. A small tear dropped down her cheek.

"We have successfully taken the castle, and now all of you. Don't bother trying to run." the man called out. "There isn't anywhere for you to go."

King Henry was crouched down in front of them, a man holding a sword in front of him. He said nothing, only sobbing into the floor.

"What do you want from us," Oliver said shakily as he stepped forward, feigning confidence.

"You're our prisoners now. Rowan will decide what to do with you."

"Fine," Oliver replied. He turned to face Ezra, a small smile on his lips. "Everything will be okay, my love."

He was once again making promises he couldn't keep. Her only chance now was that Rowan would let her live. Jarren knew her, and he knew her character. Surely he wouldn't let her be taken hostage. Perhaps he wouldn't have long ago, she worried. Now that she was married, she wasn't sure where they stood. He had been so consumed by hate and jealousy. She wasn't sure that he would listen to her reasoning. And worst of all, she wasn't sure that he would spare Oliver. Her husband, her love, was going to die.

# 27

# Arabella

Clanging of swords rang out from the church as they hurried out. Arabella and her guards poured out into a small street with a small horse-drawn wagon waiting for them. A few of the Black Cloaks surrounded them, walking their horses back and forth as they waited for her.

"Wait here. I'll be back with Henry," her guard said as he turned away.

"No. Leave him here," she said firmly.

At least if she was being forced to leave the city, she would be able to get rid of Henry, she thought. Maybe some good could come of this battle.

"But..."

"Stop. I am the Queen. I ordered you to leave him. Now let's go," she commanded.

He nodded slightly before joining her in the wagon. She watched silently, glaring out the window at the familiar brown houses she had stared down at for years. Concerned faces peered in as the carriage passed, traveling quickly across the uneven and crooked streets. Walls of tan and brown whirred past, stirring on the feeling of nausea rising in her throat.

She sat back in her seat as they approached the massive wall of gray outlining the city, rubbing her face in her hands. The carriage paused as the gate opened, and she turned back one final time. She watched as the wall grew further from her, the bodies inside growing smaller until the gate closed behind her, obstructing her view completely.

She huffed and turned to face the front as the carriage smoothed onto the door road heading north. Green mossy branches protruded from the side of the road, sticking into the path as they rode past. A small glimmer of a smile warmed her face as she caught sight of the green encompassing her. It had been so long since she had been outside of the walls. She had almost forgotten what it was like to be in the trees instead of simply looking down upon them.

"How long will it take us to arrive to Ulster?" she asked annoyedly.

"We'll have to stop tonight and rest, we should arrive by nightfall tomorrow."

Her head swirled with anger at the thought of abandoning her position as the Queen. She had tasted power, and she was not going to let it go, she decided.

"My life has been riddled with sorrow and grief. I have recently lost my husband and my son. I stand before you, broken and scarred by acts of evil. These unexpected deaths have left me and Vaor in mourning. As we are left here to pick up the pieces of this unspeakable act against my husband, the culprits rejoice in our suffering. In the wake of these tragic incidents, I vow my revenge upon the traitors who committed these crimes against us all.

We will scour the streets and leave no door unturned until the people responsible have been put to death! We will search meticulously every inch outside these walls to end the traitors indefinitely! I will not let this unspeakable act bury us in grief. We will prevail even stronger than before and put an end to the traitors living among us. I will not rest until each of their bodies are burning away into nothing! I will not rest until these streets are clean of treason! I will not rest until Vaor rises to its former glory as the strongest Port in the North! We will once again be a symbol of power and strength to all those who gaze upon us! We will not waver in the face of opposition, and we will return to our status as an untouchable force to all those who oppose!" she shouted.

The nobles all around her roared with applause as she stood alone in front of them. She soaked in their praise and admiration as she breathed in a feeling of uncontrollable power. This time, she had done it. She was the sole ruler of Vaor. She would use her father's army to take back her kingdom. She could be stopped by no one, nor would she. She would do whatever it takes to keep her power, to keep this feeling. No one would stand in her way. They would kneel before her or lie in a grave.

Lord Percival stepped through the entrance and Arabella's eyes adjusted to the dark room inside. She squinted at the low lighting and saw that the room was mostly bare, with a small bed in the corner and chains lying on the floor. They twisted around before clanging onto the wrists of a wiry woman dressed in dark clothing with long gray hair that hung down and dragged across the floor.

The woman turned to face them at the sound of their footsteps entering the room. Her face was sickly and pale, her skin sagging down from her thin, bony face. Her right eye was sewn crudely shut with thick black wire, and her lips were drawn down into a thin frown. Arabella shuddered at the sight of her, immediately stepping back from the creature.

"What is this?" Arabella asked fearfully, horror and disgust clear on her face.

Percival turned to face them, a slight smile on his face. He raised his hand to show them the small scars littering his arm. She backed away and gasped at the sight of his skin riddled with cuts. The woman began creeping closer to them, her body twisting and bending in inhumane ways. She lifted her wrinkled, pasty white palm up to Arabella who was standing in front of her, completely frozen and wide-eyed.

"What is she?" she trembled quietly.

"She's a gift from The Raven," he replied quietly, the corners of his mouth turning upward slightly and a demonic gleam shining in his eyes.

"Why do you have her here? What does she want from me?" Arabella asked as she turned to face him, fear in her eyes.

"She wants your blood," he replied with a grin.

"Why?" she shuddered, staring at the figure before her.

"One drop of blood is all it takes. One drop, and she'll tell you pieces of your future."

He handed her a small blade, gesturing to her hand.

She dragged the blade harshly across her skin, and dark red blood poured from her tan flesh, rising up to pool on her palm. She winced slightly before lowering the dagger and holding her hand out to the figure before her.

The woman took her hand and closed her left eye, smearing the palm across her face before dropping to the floor. She remained crouched against the cold stone ground, her face staring down at the floor. Her body swayed slightly back and forth, jerking harshly every few seconds as she stayed silent.

"I see death and violence in your future. Cruelty and suffering," she croaked as she stood and slithered closer, gripping tightly onto Arabella's arm, "You will struggle greatly in the war to come. You will betray those you love to regain your throne, and you will rise to power again, but at a terrible cost. One so terrible you would stop it if you could. But, the course has already been set. No one can stop it now... Death will come for us all."


The End